Digitarum

Derek Bailey

Edited by Robin Bailey

<u>Author's Note:</u>

This is a work of science fiction and fantasy. All characters, locations, and events are products of the author's imagination and any connections that can be made to the real world are up to the reader's interpretation. This is a story that draws inspiration from numerous mythologies which belong to a diverse selection cultures and belief systems from ancient times to present day and aims to incorporate them respectfully while also creating an original piece of fiction. Opinions of the various characters within this story do not necessarily reflect those of the author and are only in place to flesh out the characters in a way that best fits who they are.

Dedication

A special thanks goes to my mom, Robin Bailey for assisting this project through offering advice, encouragement, editorial feedback, and emotional support. Without her help, completing this book would have been a far more daunting, lengthier, and less enjoyable process. She's always been an honest critic as well as my biggest fan. She homeschooled me until my freshmen year in high school and continues to be my teacher in all things so it is safe to say that a lot of what I know comes from her. She has always been there to push me towards excellence and it is my goal to someday reach it. She's invested countless hours into both this book and my life in general and there is not much else to say other than that I love her very much.

TABLE OF CONTENTS

ACKNOWLEDGMENTS

While this novel is an independently published work, there are a number of individuals who are owed thanks for seeing it through to completion and for ensuring that it was released at the best possible quality. Without their assistance, the final product would not have been the same – they are as follows:

Kat Maloney: For providing feedback and artistic council on the cover image.

Jessica Dugas: For offering comprehensive advice toward the marketing of and social media support for this work.

Aaron Harrison: For contributing early feedback and editorial advice as well as reviewing the final layout of the finished work.

Joseph Umali & Co.: For unrivalled consultant services.

Out of Nothing

Darkness filled the great void. Nothing moved or made a sound. Only one tangible object inhabited the empty space – a single portal whose orange glow provided the only light to be found there. The swirling egg-shaped mass of light sat within a glittering bronze case which had a round top and squared off bottom and four slender, curved beams that connected it base to roof. It sat on a single floating platform overlooking the endless depths. The luminous energy made no sound and the darkness swallowed up its light before it could make it too far beyond the square platform. During this time, everything was silent and still. The tranquility dispelled only when the orange light started to twirl violently and brighten. Five figures burst out from the glowing cocoon and poured out over the platform, landing face down against the thin, transparent surface.

Their pale blue bodies writhed about like newborns as they pressed themselves against the glossy surface. Their heads started to shake about. They looked at their reflections in the shiny surface. For a while, they studied themselves curiously, unable to recognize their own faces. Eventually, they built up the coordination to stand and look around at each other, noticing right away that two distinctive types of them existed. Two of the five had bulging bosoms, slender waists, and broad hips while the other three had flat chests and bodies shaped in a more pointed fashion. They all had unique faces and possessed different heights and builds. Thin, white lines formed tiny boxes across their blue skin. As they looked down at their hands and studied the faces of one another, they realized that they were entirely comprised of these quadrilateral shapes. Attention drifted to the void that surrounded them and then to the radiant portal. As they took notice of it, a booming voice came from the swirling shape.

"Hello dear ones," the words rattled through them as the sound blared into the space.

There was a pause until a short, masculine figure with dense limbs stepped forward and answered, "Hello." He did not know how he spoke the word. Doing so felt more of a mimic than an actual thought.

"You must have many questions," the voice boomed back.

"Yes," the being replied, this time the word came from him rather than being a repeated syllable. He still wondered where it came from, but the fact that he produced it on his own encouraged him.

"I do apologize, little ones, there is much that I cannot tell you for reasons that you cannot comprehend. What you must know is your purpose. You exist for five individual tasks. You do not know what they are yet, but you will discover them in time. For now, know that you must build. The world you live in is dark and empty. Fill it with whatever you think is right. I cannot help you with this. You are the rulers of this domain now."

"Wait," the being burst out, but the light already faded to a dim glow. The five looked to each other in silence, unsure of what to do now that the voice abandoned them. Suddenly something sparked within the one who did the talking. "We will need a light," he said flatly. The others listened – nodding in agreement, but not giving any verbal reply. "It is too dark to see anything. If we are to build something we will need light," the speaker continued.

The others agreed with his logic, but then one of the curvy beings asked, "How?" Her voice rang out melodiously as she stepped forward – her wide hips swaying with each stride.

The question gave him pause and he took some time to compute the solution. For the light to be of any use, it would need to be set high enough into the dark space and it needed to be much brighter than the portal. But how could they reach there? As he examined the problem, his solid black eyes sprung to life. His body began to elevate into the air and he experienced a sensation of weightlessness. The others observed as he floated higher and higher into the dark space above, light now emanating from his hands. He ascended into the darkness until he could no longer see his companions. The creature found the situation troubling. He knew that he might not be able to find his way back. Fighting this fear, he eventually came to a halt. Holding his hands in front of him, he formed a glowing white orb that began to radiate light. The more he concentrated, the larger the sphere became and before long, it grew bright enough for him to see all the way down to where his comrades watched and wondered if he would return to them. Having accomplished his task, he descended back down to the platform.

"Can you teach us to do that?" The feminine one from before inquired. "To float through the air with such ease, that is. Please show us." The others bobbed their heads vigorously in agreement.

The being of light processed the request for a moment in search of the right explanation. "It takes only the will to do it. If you wish it to happen, just make it happen, it takes no great effort."

For a few minutes, the others contemplated this lesson. They started by leaping straight up into the air in hopes that they would continue to ascend, but they just tumbled to their knees and tried again. The light bringer looked to his companions. When none could repeat the act of flight, he moved over to the other speaker.

"Here," he offered, placing his hands under her arms and hoisting her into the air. Together they floated a little ways above the plane. "You must act like you are weightless. You must feel the way that you feel right this moment."

She gave him an understanding nod and he let go of her. To everyone's delight, she stayed floating in the air and started to flutter about on her own. The giver of light did the same for the others, though he strained to lift the largest of the five. The light bringer experienced positive pulsations when his pupils could finally float about through the sky. He watched them sail through the empty space, before he eventually realized they needed to return.

He called out, "Come back to the platform, we have more to do!" They all flew back obediently and landed in front of where he waited.

The bringer of light spoke out, "We need to come up with a way to identify ourselves. If we are going to build something together, we will need to be able to call each other by something."

They all nodded in solemn acknowledgement at this notion. The effeminate being from before came forward again. "You should be the one to name us."

This suggestion made him pause for a bit as he eyed his companions thoughtfully with his fist pressed against his chin. After some consideration, he walked up to the being before him. "Rin," he said to her as he passed. She had a round face with a perky nose, ears that clung close to her head and wide eyes. Her plump lips curled into an appreciative smile.

He approached the largest of the masculine beings who had bulging features and long, solid limbs. "Garta," he called as he continued. He proceeded over to the other feminine being who had a slim face and subtle features and called her "Rica." She stood a little shorter than Rin, with thinner body parts to match the scale as well as smaller curves. The last creature watched with scrunched eyes as the name-giver arrived at him. "Tubu" the light bringer announced. He stood a little taller than the light bringer, but shorter than Garta. Out of the three, he had the slightest build. His limbs still bubbled with musculature, but he had a smaller frame as well as a sharpness to his features that the other masculine creatures did not possess. He had a long, narrow nose, sharp eyes, and his chin came to a thinner point. The other two had thick jaws, broad noses, wide eyes and full cheeks. Tubu's face did not give the others negative pulses, but there something about his smile looked a bit different to them all.

When he finished, Rin stepped forward and asked, "What about you?"

He froze in his thoughts. "I do not know." He did not really come up with names for the others — they merely popped into his consciousness as if they were built in all along — like how he knew how to fly. When he searched for a name for himself, he could find none. He just shook his head at Rin who eyed him up and down.

"Yeb," she stated. "You are Yeb."

"Thank you," Yeb replied as he bowed his head. This name sent positive impulses through him, and brought a grin to his face. Regaining focus, he rallied the group together. "We should start by creating another place for us to stand. It should be large so that we have plenty of space to build things like the voice instructed."

The others nodded compliantly and they lifted off into the air. As they soared through the expanse, they discovered that they possessed the power to summon solid matter into being. It came in the form of hundreds — perhaps thousands — of the little quadrilaterals which formed their bodies. This matter came in a shade of shiny grey unlike the blue pieces which gave form to them. The little chips could be levitated through the empty space and pushed together to build larger shapes. They constructed a plane that stretched far into the horizon in every direction, setting it well beneath the platform that the primordial egg rested on. Seeing the monumental size of this surface, they felt positive feedback flow through them.

"We should build a tower," Yeb suggested, encouraged by their progress.

They began by pulling a section of the ground up into a large mound. The wiry lines distorted to conform to the new shape, creating a smooth and seamless elevation in the plane. Tubu began carving a spiraling path into the mound while the others summoned more of the square, greyish matter into existence. Using this material, they created the foundation of their structure – a large, round base with four doors positioned in a cross-shaped fashion so as to open up to each of the four primary directions. Each of them started making new floors in this same thick, disk shape, making sure the ceilings stood one and a half times the size of Garta. They suspended these sections in midair until Yeb found them ready to be attached to the rest of the building. When each of these floors received such approval, they stacked them one on top of the other. In this fashion, they built up their great citadel toward astounding heights – reaching a grand total of fifty floors that sat atop their wide base layer. At the top, they built up an open outlook where they carried the radiant portal down to.

With all this done, Yeb decided they should move on to constructing the tower's interior. He started by crafting a rounded platform with short walls to set the egg shape on. Three steps led up to this stage where anyone could stand before the primordial object. Then they each claimed a floor of the tower for their dwelling, except for Tubu who instead stood before the orb and stared into its swirling light. Yeb cut windows into the walls and set up miniature light orbs throughout the tower's ceilings so that light could pour into its interior. He also added balconies to some of the floors should they want to step out and look at the world. Garta constructed wall pieces to divide the four massive floors into smaller rooms to make the space seem more manageable and welcoming while Rica discovered that she possessed the ability to bring color to the otherwise dull grey of their new home. She turned the floors into a warm brown color and the walls and ceilings in a much lighter shade.

The extravagance of their new home gave them positive pulses that they decided they would call "pleasure". They also reasoned that negative feedback would be called "pain". None of them could figure out where these words came from, but they seemed fitting enough to use. Yeb departed from the tower to start forming the land like they did with the mound that they had built their tower on. Tubu looked down from the tower's top to see what Yeb did and then took responsibility for doing the opposite and carving out low areas in the surface. He made valleys where there Yeb erected mountains, low spots where Yeb put hills, and carved imperfections into the smooth surfaces that the light bringer raised up.

Garta stayed in the tower to continue his construction. He built tables and chairs, even beds, though he knew they did not need sleep. He also turned one of the many unclaimed floors into a place for planning and deliberation. He constructed a wide table that could seat three times as many bodies as they currently possessed. Rica set to adorning the land with blades of a navy blue hue. She also painted the land a creamy off-white color while Yeb and Tubu formed it to their liking. Rin set herself to a much different goal. She looked out from a balcony on one of the upper levels in the tower and saw the vast expanse of world. She felt that other people should live here to make it all feel less lonely. They could not be as powerful as them though, since that could end up doing more harm than good. They should, however be able to help build things and they would need a means of replicating so that she would not have to create hundreds of people all on her own.

She stared by making two beings, one that looked like her and Rica which she called "female." The other creature she made to look like the others and called it a "male." She formed them in the same way that they brought the land into existence, except that their bodies were not hard like the land, but rather soft. They had pale blue skin lined with the same white lines that covered everything else. They were given all the same parts as the five, but Rin needed to add an extra feature to each in order for them to be able to create others. She placed these things between the legs so as to be conveniently out of the way when not in use.

The new people that her creations brought into being would have to start off small for this replication to work. This meant that they would need a life cycle of some kind so that they would know to grow, but she did not know how to measure time. She tried asking them for their opinion, but it seemed that they did not know how to communicate. Seeing this from above, Rica flew down to bless them with speech. Doing this made the decorator pleased and she desired to show these folk other things, but did not know what they needed.

"Names!" Rin exclaimed. "They must have names just as we do." She looked to Rica who just shrugged her shoulders.

"You made them. It ought to be you that decides what they are called."

Rin turned back to her creation. "Rila," she called the female. "And Solan," she said turning to the male. The common folk grinned widely at being awarded these titles.

The lady creators observed the new species for a while and realized that they needed time to deactivate and recharge themselves. The constant light from above prevented these folk from being able to do this and they began to suffer from it. Rica and Rin agreed that the shining orb needed to be able to move somehow, but it did not have intelligence. They explained this to the couple and the masculine one stepped forward.

"I offer myself," he said. "Make me one with the light so that I might give it the knowledge to move. This way some times will be light and others dark."

Rin hesitated at this offer warning him that, "Once you are merged with the sphere of light, you will be one with it forever. You cannot speak with anyone and you will live alone."

"This is not so, I will always have company since people will know me during hours of brightness and remember me when it is dark. I will always be with my kind and I will be greatest of my entire race."

Rin could not argue with his reasoning and something did have to be done about the situation. After a bit of consideration and some discussion with

Rica, the females agreed that they would join the male with the light. They each took him by an arm and carried him into the air. He smiled widely as he drifted with them higher and higher above the ground. Eventually, they arrived at the source of light and there they merged the male's body with the orb. As soon as the two became one, the sphere began to rotate around the world they had created and the remaining creature could rest.

Seeing what his feminine companions did, Yeb flew to the edge of the world and curled the flat surface into an orb by pulling the corners together at a point. Knowing that the female would be lonely, Rin created another male to replace Rila's lost companion and named him Sulac. Yeb admired what she did while he finished up shaping the land.

"They are most pleasing and wonderful," he told her while they floated above the world's surface.

"I thank you. The males were made after you."

"That is a kind gesture," he replied.

Rin bowed her head and dipped down toward the ground. Yeb watched her as she twisted through the air with grace and poise. He looked down at the common couple who walked together across the land. Seeing these new beings gave Yeb new ideas. He set about creating a home for the two people to stay in. He did not make it as large or elaborate as their tower, but it was still big enough for them to be comfortable. He asked Rin to make more of them as he built up a village of these two-story buildings. Rica came in and started coloring the homes in vibrant primary colors with chrome borders. Garta came down from his post and began to build up walls around the town should anything harmful come there. He knew of nothing that could do them harm, but he felt compelled to protect them all the same. When they completed the village, Yeb decided to call it Taran. Tubu disappeared for a while as the others built up the start of a new civilization. When he returned, he brought strange tools with sharp edges that looked dangerous.

"What are those for?" Yeb inquired.

"They are for the people. You see, we should give these to them and have them fight. It would be great fun to watch."

"Why would we ever want to do that?" Yeb began to experience the negative feedback that they called pain.

"Well, I do not mean that we have to do it right now. I just mean when we're done building. What will we do? We cannot just build forever can we? Besides this is so boring! We do not have to have them all fight at once. We could just pit two of them against each other at a time. It would be very pleasing."

"No!" Yeb shouted, a little disoriented by his own volume. The negative impulses ran thick in his body. "These people are not for fighting, take those things away and put them somewhere that no one can find them."

Tubu looked to him with a scowl. He narrowed his eyes for a moment and then stormed off into the distance. The others saw this scene unfold and also felt negative compulsions toward Tubu. When their companion disappeared from their sight, they continued building the village. Rin named the new people that she created, but left the naming of infants to those who gave birth to them. She took note that Rila and Sulac's first baby did not grow, just as she had feared. Seeing her distress, Yeb came down to her.

"We will use Solan," he said. With each pass he makes, the people can get a little older.

"This is a good idea," she conceded. "But not Sulac or Rila," she added. "We need them to be like us in this way so that the common folk have someone like them to look to when we are not around."

"Then this is how it shall be," Yeb announced and he set about building this law into their bodies so that they could get older and the infants could grow.

Rica thought it rather ridiculous for them to not have anything to cover their bodies. She started by creating simple jumpsuits, making them out of the same polygonal material that she used to make her grass – polygons that were soft rather than hard. Then she painted them in a variety of colors. They hugged the folk's bodies snuggly, but still managed to cover up the extra parts that looked ridiculous when left exposed. Rica then decided that the five should have suits of their own. They did not have those parts to cover, but it would suit them all the same to have something to wear. She set off to do this while Yeb and Rin moved on to create another village. They journeyed to a valley beyond hills that separated the two plains. Had they known what would befall this new village, they would not have built it so far away from the tower.

Garta resumed his post at the top of their tower and kept a watchful eye over the village which lay only a small distance away. Rica busied herself with forming suits for her and the others. She learned quite a bit from making the jumpsuits for the people and she turned one of the floors of the tower into a workshop where Garta provided her with long tables, storage cabinets, dressers, hanging apparatuses, and storage compartments for any extra materials. She painted the suits in a glossy black color. For the males, she made thin, elastic pants, thick boots that came up to the calf, chrome plated gauntlets, and form fitting shirts with chrome armoring in the shapes of the torso muscles to help it conform to their figures. For her and Rin, she made similar outfits except that the shirts left the arms exposed and the chrome armor covered their feminine body shapes. She also made gauntlets with points on them to help protect the arm joints. She adorned the plating with delicate vine-like patterns that curled around the edges. Presenting them to her comrades delighted both her and the recipients of her gifts. She delivered the suits to Yeb, Rin, and Garta, but Tubu remained missing. No one had seen him since his weapons and ideas were rejected.

Darkness Rises

While everyone went about their tasks, Tubu devised a scheme. One night he snuck into Taran, the first village, and stole a green jumpsuit from one of the villager's homes. It fit him a bit loosely given his slender frame, but disguised him well enough to slip in and out without being spotted by Garta. He rallied a group of the villagers to himself with promises of glory and excitement. Tubu told them that he could make them more powerful, and that others would exist to serve them once they ascended to this new level. He appealed to their natural tendency towards adventure. Within a matter of days, he persuaded around forty adult males and females to follow him away from the village. The people looked up to and trusted him as a valiant leader. They had no knowledge of his wicked intentions. The folk followed him into a new realm of his own creation.

He overran one section of flatlands with hideous projections from the ground that branched out into numerous twisted extensions. They littered the surface, forming a cover for his dark plans. He left a path deep into the gnarled forest which led to a wide clearing. It was here that he set up two large buildings where he stashed the villagers. He led the males into one of the barracks and the females into the other. They realized too late that the doors only had handles from the outside. Tubu locked them away in this manner, only releasing them one or two at a time.

He took them out into the yard and beat them relentlessly. They buckled under his assaults, unsure of what to do. They never knew cruelty or evil until this point and it proved to be a difficult notion to process. He tied them to the twisted projections and slashed them with thin bars that he created. He dragged them into the courtyard and twisted and bent their limbs in ways that they were not intended to be manipulated. The more the villagers pleaded with him, the more pain he inflicted upon their quivering forms. When he felt as though their naïve spirits were sufficiently destroyed, he began to set two of them in a circle and force them to fight or else he would beat them himself. His abuses resulted in nearly unbearable negative impulses for the rattled villagers. These searing pulsations sent their processors into disarray.

While beating them proved to be satisfying towards his goal, he needed more. He withdrew one of the weapons that he made before – a jagged blade that glowed bright red. The very sight of it unsettled the villager who knelt down before Tubu and begged for mercy. He looked up to him with his shimmering black eyes as he pleaded, unsure what the weapon would do to his body. With a sharp grin, Tubu snatched the male by the shoulder and plunged the sword into his torso. The villager grunted with a pained expression on his face. When Tubu withdrew the sword, the villager collapsed into thousands of the miniature squares, forming a pile of dust. Even the dark blue jumpsuit that he wore disintegrated into the matter that it was formed from. After this discovery, Tubu trained the villagers on how to use the weapons and even made some of them fight to the death for his own entertainment.

Back at the second village, Yeb and Rin found it very troubling that Tubu stayed missing for so long. They travelled back to the tower to speak with Garta.

"I thought I saw a group of people headed south, but it happened at night and I could not be sure," He told them. "When I went down to the village the next day to investigate, I found that one third of the villagers went missing and that my eyes had not deceived me. I travelled for a bit in the direction I saw them leave and found a realm which could only be of Tubu's creation. Unsure of what I would find, I returned to the tower only moments before you two arrived to meet with me."

"Garta, you and I could surely face whatever lies in that forest together. Rin, you must return and complete the new village. The people there need you and it has not even been named yet."

Rica then arrived, taking note of the meeting that convened at the top of their tower. "Rica, can you keep watch from the tower?" Yeb asked her.

"What am I looking for?"

"Any ill that Tubu might be up to," Yeb stated as he and Garta took flight. Rin bobbed her head and took off in the opposite direction.

They did not know that Tubu already mobilized his now deranged forces and led them toward the second village which Rin named Ebuk. Tubu led his platoon around a mountain pass so as to avoid being seen by Rica who kept a careful watch over the landscape. When Garta and Yeb arrived at the twisted forest and discovered the empty camp, Tubu arrived at the village gates of Ebuk and began storming the defenses. They came in the jumpsuits that Rica made, but Tubu tattered them beyond recognition. His followers looked like wild savages with large portions of their blue and white-lined bodies exposed. They waved the crooked weapons that Tubu forged as they burst through the gates. Panic ensued while the Ebuk villagers fell into piles of glittering ash with each fatal stab. Rica saw the slaughter from her tower and quickly flew toward the scene. Rin watched in horror as her creations killed their kin without a second thought. Filled with negative pulsations, she charged toward Tubu who stood ready for her with an expectant grin.

She launched herself at him viscously. Her legs swung toward his face and she managed to deflect his sword arm every time he tried to take a stab at her. Eventually his weapon proved to be an unbeatable advantage. He deflected one of her blows and pinned her arm against his side. Left vulnerable, he stabbed his blade into her gut.

"Why?" She gasped out.

"Because *this* is my purpose," his brow curled over his eyes as the words came out in his hollow voice.

"No... it cannot –" she hissed as he pulled the blade out of her. She turned into the same square dust particles that the villagers fell into and was no more. Tubu did not know what the weapon would do to her, but the result pleased him immensely. With the all the villagers left in shining ashes, Tubu rounded up his forces and withdrew from Ebuk. The unprepared townsfolk never even fought back and Tubu did not lose a single one of his followers.

Rica watched in pain from above as Rin fell into dust at Tubu's hand. She arrived too late to help and without a means to defend herself, what could she really do? Regaining her logic, she flew toward Taran and ushered the villagers there into the tower. She told them that they would be safe there and explained what Tubu did to the other village. They obeyed her without question, evacuating to the holy bastion by the end of the day. When Yeb and Garta returned in a hurry, she told them what happened. Needing to see it with their own eyes, they rushed off to Ebuk and found that it had all been true. Yeb found Rin's remains, identifiable by the shining squares of her disintegrated chrome armor. He knelt beside the pile and scooped up a bit of the sharp dust in his hands. When he could tolerate the sight of it no longer, he let it fall back into the mound and turned away. The pain he experienced felt almost too immense to bear. Garta looked around at the devastation, equally distressed.

"WHY?" Yeb moaned in a high pitch.

"Where have they gone?" Garta questioned. "Is this all that truly remains of them? And if they are not here, where else might they be?"

"This is what Tubu wanted. He wished for this ruin. We have to protect the others from this. Then we come back for the people here. There must be something more that is left behind."

"Perhaps we will need weapons after all," Garta said with an odd quiver in his voice.

"No!" Yeb's volume went high again.

"It is a necessary evil. If we do not have a way to defend ourselves, then Tubu will destroy everything. He has already corrupted or killed over half of our people and he has twisted part of our land."

"You are right. It is the only way." Yeb pinched his eyes shut as he said this. He wondered if it would all just go away if his kept his eyes closed for long enough. Finding the effort to be futile, he glanced back at Garta with a grimace.

Garta nodded and the pair set off toward the tower. He converted one of the floors into a place where he could forge weapons. The guardian made an enormous silver axe for himself. He gave Rica a long, slender sword with a looped handle and presented Yeb with a pair of razor-edged boomerangs. Rica took it upon herself to decorate the weapons with golden trimming and ruby circles encrusting it while Garta forged a variety of blades to give to the villagers should the three of them fail. The guardians took their weapons in hand and checked their armor. They stood at the top of the tower with their backs to the egg as they looked into the horizon. Tubu's forces approached them with unrelenting speed. Determined to stop them, Yeb shouted, "charge!" The others followed
him faithfully as they flew down to meet the enemy forces. Seeing them, Tubu took to the air and sped toward Yeb.

The two titans clashed blades while Garta and Rica continued downward to deal with the twisted villagers. These foot soldiers proved to be little challenge for the pair save for their power in numbers. Garta chopped through them with his enormous axe while Rica stabbed, dashed and parried with her blade. Tubu's followers fell apart as the heroes laid waste to them. Rica leapt to and fro, slaying those who tried to gang up on Garta who plowed through several of the soldiers at a time with one swing of his weapon. Tubu became desperate as his forces diminished.

Yeb used his boomerangs as battle daggers, repelling the strikes that Tubu made against him. He flew about, not especially adept in the arts of destruction, throwing his boomerangs one at a time to stay Tubu's advance. He wanted very badly to defeat Tubu himself, but he proved to be too fierce a fighter for Yeb, so the light bringer decided to delay long enough for the others to join him. The tactic proved successful, as Tubu's forces were leveled before Tubu could land any blow against Yeb. Realizing his failure, the betrayer fled toward his forest, but Yeb pursued him followed by Garta and Rica. They chased him tirelessly, Yeb hurling his weapons at Tubu who deflected each attack with his jagged great-sword. Eventually, one of the boomerangs hit its target, striking Tubu in the back of the shoulder. The blow did not kill him, but it did knock the villain out of the sky. He crashed against the ground, just a few feet in front of his gnarled forest. The hole in his back that the strike left sealed shut again, but Tubu found himself surrounded. His narrow eyes widened as he shook his head.

"No, you cannot kill me! This does not end here. This is my purpose, this is my design. You cannot change it, I cannot change it, and I will not relent. I will be back, mark me, I will be back and I will be stronger. None of you can see the beauty in destruction, but I can. Oh I can see it, it is so wonderful!"

"Enough!" Yeb shouted.

"Goodbye, for now, light bringer. This is only the start of our glorious story."

"You will not get away, Tubu! We will make you pay for what you have done."

"Ah, and here begins our struggle, Yeb. You all lack the power that comes with darkness and deception. That is why you will fail to kill me this day. Fear not though, I will be back."

Before Yeb could respond, the ground began to shake as the twisted projections writhed to life. They shook the ground that they stood on so violently that the surface caved into a dark chasm. The heroes lost their footing and Tubu took the opportunity to run toward the large hole in the ground. The three heroes lay against the milky earth as they watched their betrayer charge toward the great opening. Tubu looked back to them for a moment with an almost solemn glance and then leapt into the darkness – disappearing from sight. The ground stopped shaking but the forest was gone. The group stared down into the pit, only able to see swirls of black fog. Not knowing what else to do, they flew back to the tower.

They sent the villagers back to Taran, but Garta made special preparations for another attack, if and when it should arise. He taught the people how to use weapons and he constructed stronger gates and walls, building the village as more of a fortress than a town. Yeb went about, forming natural barriers to the great chasm so as to avoid accidental discovery. With Rin gone, the people would have to be responsible for creating more of themselves and so they left Ebuk abandoned for the time being. Yeb made frequent visits there though. He collected the piles of matter – though he did not yet know what to do with it. He put each of the piles into ornate vases that Rica crafted for him and plugged the openings with transparent lids. When he tried to collect the fragments of Tubu's savages, he found that their ash turned into steaming black matter and melted any container he tried to put them into. So he levitated them to the great chasm and dumped them into it. He left Rin's debris for last, unable to acknowledge that this was all that remained of her.

"Why did your purpose have to be so short?" He whispered to the ashes as he collected her dust into a special golden urn. "You will be missed."

Then he left the village and did not return there for a long time. Rica busied herself with designing more styles of clothing and thinking of ways that they could teach the people to do more for themselves. She requested that Yeb drop deposits of resources across the land for the people to use as materials since they could not just summon matter into being like the three gods. He created mounds of the materials throughout the land and even buried some more of it beneath the surface in underground deposits. He decided that everything should have volume so he filled up the hollow lands with substance. Rica followed close behind to make sure that everything Yeb created had a color. Soon they would teach the people to use these materials, but for now they needed time to themselves so they all departed from the common folk. The citizens of Taran waved to their guardians whom they now referred to as their gods.

The gods gathered at the top of the tower once they completed the bulk of their work. "We need your council," Yeb announced standing before the orb. "Will you not answer us?" Still the primordial egg gave them no reply. "We have so many questions. Will you abandon us so easily?"

Rica and Garta's gaze fell to the floor. Eventually, Yeb gave up on trying to beseech the egg and realized that they already had the answer. "We build," he said in a quivering voice. "Fulfill our purpose and build. The people need us." Yeb's companions returned their eyes to him. He spun about with the dull light of the portal glowing around his backside and gleaning off of his armor. "We built this world up together – we have to protect it together. Tubu will return, but that is not a concern for today. We must simply be vigilant in keeping watch for him while we foster the growth of our people. Will you take a vow with me to protect them at all costs?"

"I will!" Rica and Garta proclaimed.

As they looked into the horizon of what they created together, they felt something that no one put a name to yet. They all felt a sense of loss for Rin's death, for the loss of Tubu's allegiance, and for the death of so many of their people. Despite it all, though, seeing how much they achieved and all they managed to protect, they felt this unnamed sensation pulse through them.

"Hope," Yeb stated. The others looked to him and nodded in agreement. They could do even better, they would do better.

Life and Death

When the three gods returned to Taran, they found the people still in mourning. They moped around the village, hardly even speaking to one another. Yeb realized that while he and his fellow gods felt hopeful, the common folk felt only despair. They could not see the beauty of their existence the same way the gods could.

"Come to me, good folk," the light bringer commanded. The people drearily formed a circle around their gods. "Why do you laze about in such idle sorrow?" Yeb asked them.

"Our creator has been taken from us," Sulac replied miserably.

"And so many of our kin have perished!" Rila wailed.

"We are in pain," several others groaned at once.

"We are also in pain," Yeb consoled them. "We will forever miss Rin's kind presence. But she would not want us to waste away like this. No, she would want us to march forward and continue the work that she started. You still have three gods who care for you. We will help you move past this. You will never be abandoned!"

The common folk bowed their heads and prostrated themselves against the ground. Yeb looked to his two companions who gave slight tips of their brows. The light god felt good about the future and believed that the people could turn all of this around.

"There is much that we should teach you, so rise up and let us begin." Rica announced. "We will start this together by building a statue of our fallen Rin so that you can learn the most important skill that we possess."

The people stood up and looked to their gods eagerly for instruction. Yeb summoned into being a deposit of matter which he placed in the village's center. Rica turned it into a shimmering golden color. Garta, meanwhile, formed picks so that the common folk could break it apart. The people chipped away at the massive boulder of golden material. With each swing, parts of it disintegrated into the teeny polygonal fragments. Other folk came by to scoop these shards up. They could not make them levitate like the gods did, but they possessed the capability to mold them into new shapes. The gods watched with pride as the common folk tore the deposit apart and build something new out of it. They erected a magnificent life-size statue of the fallen goddess in the town's center. They depicted her as standing tall with her hands over her armored chest. The undertaking lasted days, yet the folk never rested nor did they seem to tire of the task. They built each and every detail into the sculpture, except for the white lines that covered her skin. When it all finished, they retired to their huts and collapsed into their beds. Seeing the statue gave Rica an idea.

While the people slept, she went into their homes and removed the checkered lines that crisscrossed all over their blue bodies. She always thought the feature a distraction and liked the way

Rin's statue looked without them. When they all awoke, they praised their unmarked skin, loving that they could now look more like their creator's statue. Some were so ecstatic that they unsealed the fronts of their jumpsuits and either let them hang open, or went so far as to peel off the top part of them, leaving their chest and arms exposed while they danced about in glee. Pleased with the result, Rica then did the same for Yeb, Garta, and herself.

That day, the three gods stood apart, offering different lessons. Yeb took those who wished to build more homes and expand the village. Garta recruited folk who enjoyed tools, weapons, and combat. Rica attracted a lot of the females since they felt a strong desire to be like her. Other ladies, though, found that Rica's arts were far too delicate for their tastes and went with Yeb or Garta instead. Yeb demonstrated how to lay down a dense slab as a foundation and then how to construct strong walls from that base. He used his godly powers to execute the lesson quickly, but reassured them that they too could do this if they worked together and gave themselves a little more time. He taught them the fundamentals of design. All buildings needed a foundation, a roof, supporting walls, stairs, doors, and windows. What to put inside of these buildings should be the concern of others, however. Such matters would be handled by those who followed Garta and Rica. The lady god took her group of females and some males away from the village and into the fields of swaying blue grass.

"Look at the ground and stomp your feet against it," Rica commanded. The people did as she said and then looked to her. "How does it feel?" She asked.

"It is hard," Rila replied.

"Right, now go and stroke one of those blue blades," Rica advised.

"It is soft," Rila concluded cheerfully as she put one hand on her hip and another over her swollen belly which stretched her jumpsuit mercilessly.

"Exactly," Rica announced. "When we gods first brought matter into existence and built with it, all that we made was hard. But then Rin and I discovered that we could make soft particles. We knew this would be possible because we ourselves are made of a soft substance as are all of you. The jumpsuits you wear are soft. In order to make more things like them, you will need materials like these blades. Such a substance will not serve the builders or craftsmen because they need something solid, but it is very useful to our needs. Let us start by picking as many of these blades as we can."

The common folk dropped down to their knees instantly and plucked the soft strips from the ground. Seeing that they were a bit rough with this process Rica called to them, "Wait, not like that. Do not pluck it from the ground, if you do, it will never grow back. Instead, tear it at its base and over time a full blade will regrow."

The people did as she said and collected the blue fauna in this fashion. Rica watched them harvest her materials with great care. She knew the hard part still lay ahead. When her pupils gathered all they could hold, she sent them back to town. While they walked she flew back to her workshop in the tower and carried back the sample garments that she made for instructional purposes. The goddess rejoined her students in Taran and found that Garta and his troupe of craftsmen built them a table along with a machine which could split the grass strips into square particles. It had a tall backing with thin blades which could be dropped onto the suspended strips – the squishy bits would fall into the large bowl that sat below. Right next to it Garta set up another machine to help Rica's students loom together all the fragments into pliable strips and then to pieces of a garment. Then they could seal up each part and attach it all into whatever they knew how to make. For those more interested in crafts, the goddess showed them how to make blankets and cushions, but clothing is what really excited her. Rica showed them dresses with wide necks and tiny sleeves. She presented flaring jackets and different kinds of pants – some tight, others loose. They became students of fashion, but lamented that they only had the color blue to work with.

"I will invent more kinds of soft materials," she promised them. "They will have different feels as well as different colors." Then she left them to their studies and took off to fulfil this promise.

In the meantime, Garta showed his group how to forge more than just tables and machines. He demonstrated how to create a blade and explained the proper way to pinch the particles shut so that they came to a sharp edge. Together, they created weapons like those the gods wielded, but most preferred simple one-handed swords. The large god studied a few that walked off a little ways to swing the blades around. He realized that he would need to train two sets of people – one that would forge weapons and machines, and another that would use them. He separated those who had a fondness for using the blades and found a space for them to train outside the village walls. He demonstrated different swings and they followed his movements. Holding his mighty axe brought his thoughts back to Tubu. He left his warriors-in-training to fly off toward the grand chasm.

As he flew, he noticed that a small pack of gangly figures walked from where Tubu fled into the dark abyss. The god saw no sign of the betrayer, but the lanky creatures below gave him enough cause to fly closer. When he drew nearer, he saw that these beings had no faces, or even distinctive musculature. They possessed only the color of black upon their exposed flesh – not that they looked exposed since Garta found their bodies could not really be distinguished as parts, but rather flowed like some kind of goo. They looked like ghouls, not people and they let out horrid shrieks when they saw him arrive. He wasted no time in swiping his massive weapon at the stringy beasts. His axe cleaved through them with ease – their bodies falling into onyx ash. Three of the monsters fell to Garta's might but the god noticed that one managed to scurry away from him. Rather than charging at it head on, he decide to see where it would go, so he followed it for a ways until another twisted forest came into view. This one was smaller than the first and shrouded in bubbling, black smog. Garta watched the creature slink into the dark haze. The god did not dare follow it into the forest so he flew back toward Taran.

While Yeb supervised the construction of two new homes, he could not stop looking over to where

Rila cobbled together a white dress. At times he caught himself watching her work for too long and pulled his attentions back to the construction projects. Sulac took notice of the god's gaze and scowled in his direction. Rila took notice as well, but did not make any acknowledgement of it. She just continued to craft her garment.

In the meantime, Rica sat in her workshop within the tower and summoned different sorts of materials into being. Some of the fragments had fuzz around them, some could be stretched, some coarse, and others stringy – some shiny, some vibrant, others dull. When she created a plethora of different types of mater, she set to planting fields of it for the people to find and harvest. She made sure they could be found in a vast spectrum of colors, making some hues common and others rare just for a bit of fun. Her work was just about finished when she saw Garta soaring through the air toward Taran. She took off to see why he fled there with such speed.

When Rica arrived in Taran, she found Garta standing beside Yeb, clutching his shoulder and leaning his face toward the light bringer's ear. Garta spun about when he heard the soft patter of the goddess' landing. She looked to them with eager eyes. Yeb bowed his head to Garta who took off toward the tower. She waited while Yeb hastened over to where she stood. He looked around for a moment before leaning in.

"Head to the tower war room," he whispered.

She made no protest to his command. He watched her head back to their home and turned to find Sulac and the pregnant Rila approaching him. The lady looked to him with a raised brow.

"What is happening, Yeb?" She started. "Why do the gods whisk away with such urgency?"

"We go to discuss matters of the darkness," he admitted. "We cannot let it surprise us like before. Tell any who ask that we will return to them and that they need not fear."

"And why do we not join in these discussions?" Sulac broke in. "Are we not worthy of having a say?"

Sulac's boldness gave Yeb pause. "You are needed here among your people," Yeb soothed. "The people look to the both of you for leadership when we three are not around. We rely on that. Can we count on you to fulfill such a duty Sulac? Or shall I ask this of another?"

"No," Sulac gasped. "You will find that I am more than up to such a duty."

"Good," Yeb said with a tip of his head. "When more is decided, you will be informed."

"Be safe, Yeb," Rila added.

"And you as well," Yeb concluded while rising into the air and rocketing off toward the godly citadel.

He flew into the towering fortress and met his fellow gods on the Floor of Deliberation. The expanse of the War Room table made the hall feel desolate. They took seats at one end of the table, Yeb finding that they left the head of it for him. He took his chair and looked to Garta who rubbed his hands together.

"Tell us what you saw, my friend," Yeb invited. "Has Tubu returned?"

"Not exactly," Garta's voice boomed. "I did not see the traitor, but I did find horrid monstrosities seeping out of the dark chasm and skulking about our lands."

"Did you destroy them?" Rica jumped in.

"All but one," Garta explained. "I left one alive and followed it to where it might go. That is when I discovered another dark forest – this one teeming with a thick fog."

"How big?" Rica asked.

"It is quite small, but without being able to see into it, I cannot say how many of the creatures wandered into there."

"It is a breeding ground where dark things can grow," Yeb cut in. "To go there now would be too great a risk. We must raise our own forces and then move against it."

"So we do nothing?" Garta challenged.

"No," Yeb protested. "We continue building and keep watch on that forest. We must tend to our people, so let us return."

They arose from their seats. But before they left, Yeb turned to Garta with a grin. "We should do that more often," he said motioning to the table. The larger god looked to his grand craftsmanship with pride, noticing that Rica colored it red and gave it gold trimming.

"Hold on," Rica, sputtered before the gods departed – never having left her seat.

"What is it," Yeb asked turning back to her.

"I – I was thinking." Her voice quivered. "Perhaps I should give us those extra parts," she said hastily while looking to the other end of the table.

"For replication?" Yeb confirmed.

"Yes," she huffed.

"To make more of ourselves, replenish the ranks?" Garta clarified.

"Maybe not right away – just – it would be good – we ought to have the option." She rambled.

"Do it," Yeb agreed, bobbing his head.

"Okay," she sighed quickly, letting her shoulders fall back.

Garta went into the next room while Yeb slid out of his armored attire. She created a part of him and attached it to his pelvis. He waited silently for her to do this and dressed himself once she completed the process. Then he left for the village.

Garta came in and she gave him the additional feature. When he too left she undressed herself and placed the opposing part to theirs between her own legs. Her hands shook when she finally finished, but having this feature came as a relief to her. Long had she envied the common folk's ability to duplicate themselves. Now that but three of the gods remained, she felt that they needed to be able to do the same. They would not abuse this power, but she knew they could not do this alone. Something else drove her to this conclusion as well. Ever since their arrival into this domain, she felt strong pulsations towards Garta and longed for a way to express them.

When Yeb arrived back in the village, he found that not only were the two new homes complete, but that the common folk already began work on a new project. They created the foundation for a great hall in which the gods could stay whenever they wished. Yeb insisted that it instead be built for the two immortals, Rila and Sulac – that the gods would have rooms reserved for them, but only be honored guests there. The people did not yet understand that they would not always get to just be citizens of Taran. There would be far more to build and new places for life, but for now they simply accepted Yeb's council at its face value. When Garta arrived, he expanded the village walls at the requests of the villagers. They knew they could do so themselves, but that would take much time and they wanted Taran to grow quickly. Garta completed the task whole-heartedly – expanding the walls to create ten times the space that existed before. He hoped this might be enough to keep them occupied for a time.

Back at the tower, Rica stayed locked away in her workshop. She discovered a way to improve appearances even further. During her experimentation, she came upon a way to create, thin, cylindrical cords. They could be pulled straight or pushed up into waves. They could even be spun into curls. She thought it might be a fine thing to have such a material come out of people's heads so she tried it on herself. The dark fibers looked marvelous against her pale blue skin and abyssal eyes. She found that she could make this material any color she wished, but felt that black, white, yellow, and different shades of brown looked the best when held against her face. She delighted at how it could be shaped in nearly any way and that it could grow like her blades of grass. She then diced up some of the cords into tiny bristles and speared them over her brow into two arching curves. The result pleased her greatly and she decided that all should have these fine features to enjoy, but she had one more experiment to conduct. She took bits of hard, white material and put it into a bowl which she then held over one of Yeb's light orbs that she stole from her ceiling. The radiance of the orb heated the bowl, but not enough. She invigorated its energy until the fragments grew hot enough to melt into a paste. She then dipped her fingers into it and smeared some over her lips and around her upper eyelids. The result pleased her, but she wanted to save this look for a particular occasion, so she wiped the paint off of her face with a cloth and took the rest with her.

She returned to Taran to find the new keep completed. Her students marveled at the brown fibers that fell from her head. She offered to give them some to enjoy and they agreed readily. They each started with long, flowing locks, but she showed them how easily they could be cut and shaped. If they found they did not like it short, they need only wait for it to grow back. She also gave them eyebrows of matching color. She did this for the entire village, making it so that newborns would enjoy this gift from birth. Then she bestowed it upon Yeb and Garta. She gave Yeb some with a white hue to match the white light that he put into the sky. Then she gave Garta black locks to honor his skill in slaying servants of the darkness. Together they watched as the civilization grew. Garta received permission to devote his time to training interested males and females. After a while, he found that a group of four females split off and began training on their own. He watched them for a time and noticed that they used unorthodox techniques in their fighting, most of which involved manipulating their opponent more than using a weapon. Their art seemed a bit unrefined to Garta, but still elegant in a way.

"Why is it you have left my training?" the god asked.

Mili, the most assertive of the four stepped forward. "Each of the gods are teaching us," she said. "Everyone but Rin has this chance. We want to devote our studies to her so that her memory will always be kept alive by our people. She laid down her life in defense of our kind, and we think it only right that we do the same. We want to call ourselves the Daughters of Rin."

"This is a noble goal," Garta admitted. "I know you shall make her proud."

"Thank you," Mili answered with a beaming grin and then she returned to leading their training.

Rila brought another being into the world and cared for it with much pride. Yeb did not know how many children she bore, but knew that she contributed much the village's population with Sulac's assistance. After this child, though she seemed to be tired of bearing newborns and often he saw her avoiding Sulac so that she could busy herself with creating new dresses. She had black hair now which she shaped into rippling waves that bounced about when she walked. Yeb could not say what precisely about her demanded so much of his attention, but he found it difficult not to look at her. One day he approached the immortal while she worked at splitting materials and weaving them together.

"Would you care for a walk, my lady?"

"I would prefer to work, Yeb, but I will walk if my god commands it."

"I would command nothing of you," Yeb assured her. "I did come with something to ask."

"And what is that?" she inquired wither her hands still busy at the cloth-working station.

"I long for a child."

"A child?"

"Yes, I – well I would like for you to bear one for me."

"Yeb," she snapped spinning about to face him. "I have been bearing children for as long as I have lived. It is not my wish to create any more, unless of course you choose to command it."

"No, but I wish you would reconsider. It is but one more child. That is all I ask. And I could reward you. I could give you a home in the tower, perhaps even make you into a goddess."

"I have no use for an eternity in that tower, nor do I care for the power of a god," she replied. "But I care for you," she admitted. "And I pity your loss. I know you would have had such beautiful children with Rin, but it seems Tubu took much from us all. I would give you that which was denied you, but the child may or may not be born a god. In either case, I would not let them live like one. I would want our baby to live with the people, receiving no special favor from the gods, is that clear?"

"If you did this for me, I would grant you anything you wished," Yeb promised as he took her hands into his and stared into her eyes. "May I persuade you to stay with me in the tower until the infant is born?"

"Just until they are born," she agreed.

Rila finished up the red dress which she toiled away at and then let Yeb carry her off to the tower under the light of a setting sun. In the village stood Sulac. He peered out at them – his hands curled into tight fists at the sight of Rila flying off with the god.

In the great hall, Rica reapplied the white paint to her lips and eyes. She also drew white swirls down her cheeks and around her neck. She slipped into a white dress which cut down her chest deeply – exposing much of her petit bosom. She tugged her hair straight, letting it fall over her shoulders. A golden necklace hung around her neck and she clamped earrings with dark blue encrustments around her earlobes. Then she crept into Garta's chamber and slowly shut the door behind her. The dim light reflected off of her brilliantly as she approached the half undressed Garta who looked to her in complete stillness.

"I do not wish to explain myself," she started. "I merely feel strong pulsations to be with you tonight. I want to create something with you that is unlike anything we have created thus-far. I want to make something special with you."

Garta stepped over to her and cupped his hands around her face. "We want the same things," he promised before locking his lips with hers.

Keeper of Time

Yeb set Rila down onto the dark brown flooring of his section of the tower. He himself had not spent much time there since the tower's completion. Garta turned the floor into a magnificent set of various chambers, most of which had no furnishings. He led her into the bed chambers which contained a mammoth, roofed bed with drapes hanging around each of the four supports. Tall wardrobes and long dressers lined the walls along with plush, curvy chairs and glistening, white end-tables. Rila inched around, dumbfounded by the extravagance of the space.

"I have many empty rooms," Yeb started. "I could turn one of them into a place for you to make your clothing. I'll make sure you always have enough materials to work with."

"I do not intend to make this my home," she reminded him.

"I know, but giving life to a child can take some time, I want you to be comfortable while you stay here."

"You go to much trouble to have one of the common folk bear your child. Are you quite sure you wish to do this with me? I have no wish of disappointing a god."

"There is nothing common about you," Yeb replied – watching her as she explored the chamber. "I have no expectations for this child. My ambitions are merely to have a child to call my own and you are the only person I wish to do that with."

"Now that you no longer have Rin, that is." She twirled back around to face him, her loose, green dress billowing around her legs.

"There is much of her in you," Yeb admitted. "I do not mean to replace her. I just want to move on."

"I understand you, Yeb. I meant no accusation. I promised you a child and a child you shall have so long as you are prepared that it might not be born like you. And if you promise again to allow me to raise it among the people – to let us live a normal life."

"As I promised before, I now promise it again."

She bowed her head for a moment, eyeing the sumptuous bedding. "Wait there," she commanded. "If we are to do this, I will make it special for us both." She walked over to him and snatched up the red dress which he held for her. "Do not disrobe yet." She left the warmly colored room, her pointy shoes clicking against the hard floor.

Yeb took a seat at the foot of the bed and awaited her return. She entered through one of the bedroom doors wearing her rippling hair over her shoulder and the tight, red dress. Its wide neck left much of her shoulders exposed and the tiny sleeves revealed her slender arms. The stretchy fabric flowed around her bulging breasts, hugged her narrow abdomen, curled over her round hips, and fell down her legs. She walked over to him with bare feet and swaying hips. He stood up and she reached for the bottom of his plated shirt – peeling it upward and off of him. She ran her hands down his broad chest and leaned in for a kiss. He took her by the hand and led her to the side of the bed where he picked her up in his arms and set her down on the squishy mattress. Then he climbed on top of her and the kissing continued for a while until they saw fit to remove the rest of their clothing.

In Taran, Garta watched with concern as two of his warriors slowed in their movements. At first, he assumed that he worked them too hard, but then he discovered that they were not recovering. Rica noticed a similar affliction among elder members of the townsfolk. One night, when they lay together – covered only by the bed sheets, they discussed the matter.

"The people are ill," Rica sighed.

"I cannot say what is causing such suffering," Garta added.

She rolled over to face Garta and grasp his bulging arm. "It is as though the life in them is fading."

"Perhaps there is such a thing as growing too much," he mused.

"We will need to convene with Yeb on this, then."

"Agreed, let us leave in the morning."

"And tonight?"

"Tonight, we could repeat that which we engaged in last evening."

"Perhaps we do it a little differently," she suggested, climbing over him under the covers.

Garta grinned a little. "Different can be good," he agreed.

The next day the pair flew from Taran and made for their home. Yeb awoke beside Rila who now had the spark of life within her once again. He arose from the bed and walked onto his balcony. Off in the distance, he saw the others approaching, so he hastened back into his room and threw his armored clothing on. Rila's eyes opened as she heard Yeb rush up to the War Room. He entered just as Rica and Garta came through the doors.

"What brings you here with such speed, my friends?"

"The people are not well," Rica explained.

"What has happened?" the light bringer asked with wide eyes.

"We think some have grown too old," Garta lamented. "We do not know what to do."

"Perhaps such beings were not meant to live forever," Yeb concluded. "Perhaps after enough time, they ought to die."

The others shifted uneasily. "Must they?" Rica inquired. "Perhaps we could just turn it off after a while, make it so that they stop growing."

Yeb contemplated this for a bit. When he found no answers, Rila's voice cut the silence. "It is not such a blessing to live forever," she told them. "For people to die means that pains of the past may be forgotten. Take this from someone who knows. You gods are preoccupied with the present and the future. Your abilities make it so that you do not share in the idle toils of the common folk. We must face our own thoughts during times of quiet and after a while, these thoughts grow bitter with bad memories, and perhaps regret. Look at Sulac. He is defiant toward you because he is plagued by the pains of times past. I understand why you wish for he and I to stay as we are, but imagine if everyone was this way."

"So you think it is better if people die?" Rica asked bewildered.

"I know it to be so." The gods looked to her while they processed what the immortal said.

Rila left them to consider her opinion. Her testimony left them in a state of confusion. They did not think death could ever be a good thing, but it certainly seemed better than aging to the point of utter uselessness. They also began to fear the loss of the people's affections. What would they do if the common folk ever rejected them? Who would they care for? How would they spend their eternities?

"It will be done," Yeb announced. "But if we do this, we will need someone to look after time. It will become an important part of the people's lives and it must be cared for. Someone must also see to the collection of their ashes, for they cannot be simply left to lie around. We three have not the time to do this, but perhaps one of the people can. Maybe one of them can be made into one of us, but they must be different from their kin somehow."

"I know of one," Rica offered. "There is a male who never seems to leave his home. No one goes to visit him and it is a rare thing to see him come out into the village. Perhaps he is the one that we seek."

"It is possible," Yeb agreed. "But how will we change him?"

"Leave that to us," Rica said. "We will confront the egg until it answers us."

"Very well, I shall return once I find what we need."

With this, Yeb left the hall and flew from the tower. Rica and Garta ascended to the towers top where the portal sat enshrined. Rica stepped up onto the podium and called upon it in hopes that the voice might answer.

"Great spirit, long have you been silent, but we have a question which must be answered." When no reply came she continued. "We must know if one of the common folk can be made to be like us." Again, no reply came. "Is there a way? If so, then we must know it." Still the swirling light did not come to life and answer them. "We will have our answer no matter how long it takes."

Suddenly the light brightened and a voice thundered into the air. "You are persistent, indeed. You may have your answer. Should you wish to transform one of your creations into one like yourself, place them into my energy and I will return them to you as such a being." Then the light faded and the voice disappeared before it could be thanked.

In Taran, Yeb sought out the man that Rica spoke of. Sulac saw the god arrive and left his work to confront him. He stormed over where Yeb landed.

"Sulac," He called cheerily.

"Yeb, my dear brother-god." Sulac replied through a slim grin and a strained voice. "You have returned to us, are you here to help with the suffering?"

"May we speak alone, honored one?"

The god's flattery brought a genuine smile to Sulac's face. He relished in the god's desire to have a private council with him despite feeling wronged by him. He knew all the people in the village would see them sneak into a private place. He would be looked to as one who holds secret discussions with the gods.

"Yes," he bellowed. "Please, join me in the hall."

Sulac threw his hands wildly toward the building which sat at the heart of the village and stepped gallantly as he led the god toward its steps. Sulac threw open the door and held it ajar for Yeb to enter. Before he shut it behind him, he poked his head out to make sure plenty saw them. He found that many did indeed watch which pleased him immensely. He stepped into the assembly room where Yeb waited.

"I have come with a cure that may be upsetting to some."

"How could a cure be upsetting?" Sulac inquired with his head cocked to the side.

"The cure is to die. I come granting death. The bodies of the common folk are not meant to live forever, not like yours or mine."

"Do you not consider me one of the common folk?" Sulac asked with a pitchy voice.

"No, my friend. You may not have powers, but you and Rila are just as special as the gods."

"Is that why you took her?" He challenged.

"Yes," Yeb said patiently. "I need her help and she will return once she has lent me her aid."

"I see," Sulac huffed. "So death then, that is the answer, but how can that be so? Is death not an evil?"

"It is if one is corrupted by Tubu," Yeb allowed. "But for those who remain true to the gods, there is nothing to fear from death. We keep the ash of those who have fallen with us. For the rest of eternity, the dead may be with their kin and with the gods. We protect our people, even in death."

"And this is why you sought to speak with me?"

"Not quite, there is more." Yeb paused for a moment. "I am told there is a male here that keeps to himself, one that who rarely leaves his home. Could you direct me to him?"

"Teylaan? What could we possibly do for you? He is a hermit, a madman."

"We are in need of someone to keep time and take care of the dead. We intend to make him a god."

Sulac stepped back and gasped – hurt that the gods did not so much as consider him for such a position. He steadied himself, knowing now could hardly be the right time to stand against a god. He could still play this to his advantage. If he stood against Yeb, all of his newfound fame would disappear, but if he aided the god now, perhaps Yeb would return for more council later. What hurry did he have after all? He being an immortal had an eternity to build up his status. He need only be patient and accommodating to Yeb's wishes.

"Does this displease you, Sulac? Do you recommend another?"

"No," the immortal exclaimed. "No, Teylaan might be perfect for your needs, dear Yeb. You need only know that he is quite odd. But I have heard that when he does go out and about, he is always rambling about the days, always uttering strange statements about time."

"That is exactly what I seek!" Yeb proclaimed with joy and clapped Sulac on the shoulder. "Please take me to him."

Sulac forced a smile and led Yeb out of the Great Hall. He sauntered through the streets once more with the god at his heels. To lead a god along like this gave Sulac immeasurable pleasure. To have such a captivated audience only elated him further. They arrived together at a small, one-story home. Sulac climbed the short steps to the hut's front door and rapped against it.

"Teylaan, do come out, the bringer of light has need of you." When no answer came, Sulac gave the god a brief smirk and threw open the door for him. "Do go on, he is a strange fellow, probably muttering something to himself, just go on in, you are his god, he will not mind."

Yeb bowed his head to Sulac and proceeded up the steps. Before going into the dwelling, he placed a hand on the immortal's shoulder and leaned his face toward Sulac's ear. "Rila worries that you have grown bitter from pains of the past. You must know that you always have the love and respect of the gods. We hold you very dear, no matter what."

Sulac saw this as the most perfect opportunity presented to him yet. He threw his arms around the god in a tight embrace. "Of course I do, my beloved friend." He let Yeb go and indulged him with a deep and slow bow at his waist. "My love for you is unending, dear Yeb. Please come to me again with anything I might help with."

"Thank you, Sulac." Yeb said softly. He beamed at the immortal and entered into the house, shutting the door behind him.

Sulac proceeded through the gawking crowd with his chin thrust high up into the air. He felt all of the eyes resting upon him. He knew the folk would be impressed by his relationship with the god and that they would find his humble service touching. A deep pain pulsed through him, but the satisfaction he felt in this moment drowned it out.

Yeb walked through Teylaan's narrow grey hallway. He could hear a faint mumbling and a scraping coming from one of the rooms. When he entered into the sitting area – which the owner sparsely littered with chairs – he found his folk. Teylaan scurried back and forth uttering inaudible phrases to himself. His blue body was stark naked – the male not even making the effort to cover his dangling parts. He also seemed entirely unaware of Yeb's presence. So Yeb observed the madman for a bit and walked a little closer to the table that Teylaan took his knife to every now and then. He noticed that the crazed male carved squares into the tabletop and put odd markings in the top corner of each.

"What is this," Yeb inquired.

Teylaan's squinted gaze turned to the god without any surprise, making it seem like he knew of Yeb's presence all along and merely chose not to acknowledge it. "Oh – yes this. This is it – I think. It must be – yes this is the answer." He sputtered.

"I am not sure I understand you."

"It is simple, you see." Teylaan started pointing erratically to the table. "The light comes and the light goes. Each time that happens, it is a day. One day includes one light, then one dark. When light comes again – new day. There are three hundred – no three hundred and sixty days, then we get older. Every day we are older, but every three hundred and sixty, we are a new age. But that is hard to remember – we must split it – split it by four – that is a cycle.

They split each of those by three – that is easier, yes. No – it's also hard to remember. Need to write it down – need to keep it safe."

Yeb looked to the person with unease. The claims of his madness were not exaggerated, but still this male seemed perfect, despite his shortcomings at communication. Yeb decided he could talk to this folk – he just needed to speak the right language.

"How would you like to study this forever?" Yeb offered. "We need someone to become a god and take care of time for us – someone to monitor the lives of the common folk and care for those whose time is over."

"Yes, let me!" Teylaan practically shouted. "I will do it, I can do it, let me do it."

"Well, let us get you started then, but first please do cover yourself with something."

"What? Clothes – oh yes, people want me to wear those. Do I have to?"

"It is part of the job," Yeb persuaded.

Teylaan bobbed his head rapidly and raced through his home in search of garments. Then he returned wearing baggy red pants and a long green coat and tall, black boots. He looked rather ridiculous, but Yeb found it more pleasing than the alternative.

"Will you take nothing else with you?" Yeb asked. "You're home will be in the tower now."

"I have clothes, I am ready," Teylaan huffed.

The god shook his head and scooped up the male. He walked him out into the day's light and flew him away to the tower. Rica and Garta waited at the tower's peak. When Yeb arrived with Teylaan, they brought him up to the portal and guided him to the spinning energy. Teylaan stood transfixed for a moment, before tearing his clothing off and leaping inside of it. Inside of the swirling mass, Teylaan felt power surging through his body and a warmth – accompanied by distorted images of a strange looking city made of gold. The gods stood and waited for a while until Teylaan finally sprung out of the orb and crashed to the ground. They gods could feel power emanating from his reborn body. They helped him up and redressed him.

"He'll need a place to stay, and another to work." Rica stated.

"No," Yeb corrected. "Make them one in the same. He hardly relaxed as a common folk and something tells me he will not get much use out of a domestic floor as a god."

"Very well," Rica stated. "Shall we get to work then, Garta?"

The large deity bobbed his head with a grin and they began to march into the tower.

"Use the one right below here," Yeb suggested. "That way he can also listen for the voice."

They dipped their brows in acknowledgment and carried on. Teylaan wandered over to the chest-high wall where he peered out over the horizon.

"I can learn much here," Teylaan mused.

"Yes, but for now, see to it that your new home is built to fit your needs. I must go back to Taran and set something new into motion."

With that, Yeb took off once more as darkness started to fall. He made it halfway to the town when all light left the night sky. That is when he lit the way with his hands. He dimmed them when he came upon the village, not wanting anyone to see him. He stood at the town's center for a bit, staring into the light of his palms. He did not know that Sulac watched from his bedroom window. He did not know how the people would respond. He did not even know if this would prove to truly be the best solution. Then he set aside his fears and cast death upon all except Sulac, Rila, and the gods. Each of the common folk now lived on a timer and once that timer reached its end, they would return to the fragments from which they were made. Time no longer came in an unlimited supply. It needed to be kept and cared for. It needed to erase the troubles of days past. With Teylaan in their ranks, Yeb felt confident that time would be on the gods' side.

Law and Order

Teylaan remained surprisingly focused for the duration of his floor's construction. Garta sectioned off a small area where he placed a bed, end-tables, a wardrobe, and some shelves. Despite being fully aware that Teylaan would likely not spend much time there, Rica still busied herself with giving color and comfort to the space. She knew right from the beginning that this floor would be very different from the others so she veered away from the warm browns and reds, in favor of some darker, cooler colors. She stained the floors with a deep purple and the walls with an indigo blue and trimmed it all with a mellow silver rather than sparkling gold. Garta covered three quarters of the remaining space with shelves that stretched from ceiling to floor which he arranged in rows. Rica then covered them with a shiny black hue. This is where they stored the remains of the fallen. Rica crafted enough copper-colored Jars to fill every aisle. The empty ones sat without lids while they capped the filled ones so as to distinguish them from the others. Garta brought down the already filled urns that Yeb collected after the first great battle and gave them to Teylaan who put them neatly away.

While they continued to arrange the new floor, Yeb went to Taran and collected the ashes of the first ten folk to die of natural causes. The old and weary could now rest for eternity. Yeb scooped up their ashes into Rica's containers and placed them into a crate. The people gathered around Rin's statue waiting for the god to explain himself. When Yeb emerged, he saw the folk's sullen faces and could not help but feel responsible for the deaths of their loved ones. He paused before them with the crate in hand.

"Your friends and family come with me now. They go to gain eternal rest from the toils of life and to be with their ancestors. They come home to live with their gods and you will all join them some day. Death will come to us all eventually, let Rin's statue remind you of this. To die at the end of a blade is a regrettable end, but to die in one's bed around those who care for you is a beautiful thing."

The crowd nodded and mumbled silently. Yeb departed from them – leaving the folk to consider his words. Sulac peered into the horizon as the god disappeared.

While Yeb collected the villagers' remains, the others finished loading up the shelves. Teylaan received the new jars and catalogued them in his mortuary. Yeb saw that Teylaan developed a new type of material similar to that which Rica summoned. This matter flapped loosely, but did not feel soft. The Keeper of Time used a brush and melted black matter to paint symbols onto the flimsy sheets.

When Yeb looked over Teylaan's shoulder, the Keeper told him, "I am recording the names of each of the fallen males and females along with their locations here. I can teach you to all to read these symbols once I have the alphabet finalized."

When a sheet filled up, he stuck the pages into a great binding to hold them all together and allow him to flip through them. He placed this ledger on one of the large tables that Garta made. These workbenches all stood in a great circle and Teylaan already started to fill them with his papers and utensils.

"This is good – yes most good," Teylaan announced. "Leave the rest of this place empty – I want to fill it now."

All the gods did as the Keeper wished and left him to his work. First, Teylaan constructed a transparent orb. It showed him images of anything in the world that he wished to see. He used it to monitor the dying and see when they met their life's end. Then he flew to Taran and brought them back to his grand crypt. Eventually, he no longer needed to watch them through this ball. He instead created a massive scroll of all those who lived. It marked when they entered into the world as well as when they would leave it. This scroll did not work like his other writings, however. When he crossed a name off of the scroll, the name went away for good, leaving him with only those who still lived. The scroll also arranged these names for him in order of age. Those closest to death lay at the top and those new to life could be found at the bottom. Every day, Teylaan checked and edited this scroll so that he knew who he needed to gather. His calendar became a huge assistance in this effort so he created a massive version of it and placed it upon his back wall where he could look to it from any of his workstations.

While Teylaan grew in proficiency as the Keeper of Time, both Rica and Rila grew with child. Rica no longer had a floor to herself, instead she moved onto Garta's floor, taking her many wardrobes with her. This left her old floor empty so Yeb and Garta turned it into a place of relaxation. Rica's old bedroom became a mammoth lounge with plush couches, chairs, and mats set up throughout the space. The gods and Rila enjoyed spending some time together here while the infants grew inside of their mothers. Rica and Rila, in particular got much use out of this chamber of comforts. They talked at great length together in this room. Rica's vigor towards motherhood made Rila feel quite excited herself, despite having done this many times before. She envied Rica's ability to bear the child without much pain or even discomfort. All of that changed one day when the goddess's baby was nearly ready to be born. In the middle of a conversation, Rica shrieked in agony. Her cries echoed through the tower at such a pitch that Yeb and Garta could hear it a few levels below where they worked on the construction of a training floor. Garta burst into the room where Rila stroked the goddess hair and tried to calm her. When neither she nor Garta could make the pain subside, they brought her up to the primordial egg and called upon it desperately.

"Great voice, do not delay this time, we are in need of your help immediately." Garta's booming voice flooded the space around them.

"What matter demands my intervention this time?" the echoing voice called out as the swirling lights sprung to life.

"There is something wrong with our baby! Rica – she's suffering and we do not know how to stop it."

"I see," the voice hummed. "To birth a god-infant must be no small matter. Cast her into my light so that I might help her deliver it."

Yeb and Garta helped the wailing Rica out of her maternity gown and into the portal. Rila stood behind anxiously as the lights flashed in a brilliant display and a vibration rattled through the air. Inside of the egg, Rica felt an overwhelming warmth and beheld hazy images of a golden city. Rila, Yeb, and Garta waited there for a long while until the commotion finally settled and out of the swirling energy came Rica, holding a squirming baby boy in her arms. Garta rushed up to her and wrapped them in his embrace.

"What should we call him?" she whispered through a smile.

"How about Timku?"

"I like it." Her eyes could not be drawn from the wiggling body. "Would you like to hold him?"

Garta nodded and took Timku up in his arms. While he cared for the infant, Rila came up and helped Rica back into her gown. Then Rica retired with Garta to their room to enjoy their newborn babe. Rila delivered her little boy shortly after and named him Manuun. Yeb and Garta built cribs for their sons together, and then returned to their families and did not see each other again for a while. Yeb delighted in beholding his son. Seeing the god play with the infant made Rila want to linger a bit longer in the tower than she initially intended. Eventually though, when the child slept one night, she came up to Yeb who stood looking out into the evening skies. She put a hand against his back and another around his shoulder. She rubbed the smooth fabric of his dark green tunic.

"He is beautiful," Yeb mused.

"Yes, he is," she replied softly.

"You are ready to leave."

"I am."

"Just a while longer," he pleaded. "Let me make you a new home, find you a fine place to live out your days."

"I think I can allow that," she giggled.

"You do not *have* to leave you know."

"I know that, Yeb, but this child needs to live among his people, as do I."

"I understand," Yeb said looking downward. "I will go in the morning then."

"Thank you," she replied sliding her hands off of his loose shirt. "Come to bed with me tonight." She led the way back to the bed with the baby crib now sitting next to it. They climbed under the sheets together and Yeb lay there with her until she fell asleep, then he sat up to see his sleeping baby. The fact that he slept told Yeb that Manuun was indeed at least partially like his mother. This came as no surprise, yet he wondered if the child inherited anything from him since even Manuun's hair shared the same black color as his mother's.

The following morning, Yeb looked out at the world from the top of the tower. In the months that passed during the pregnancies, the common folk developed Taran into a bustling city. Adventurous spirits even split off to develop two new villages called Arket and Kinam. The sprawling Taran dwarfed these infant settlements, but they seemed like they might offer the best chance for Rila and Manuun to avoid much scrutiny over being family to a god. So he flew to Arket which had no walls built around it yet. The town consisted of a large hall like the one in Taran as well as a homes of all sizes built up around it. No golden statue stood at its heart, but Yeb liked the simplicity of this place and found that the idea of new villages pleased him. Expanding civilization was always the goal, but after the destruction of Ebuk, it seemed so far out of reach for a time. These towns would be far safer than Ebuk, though. The three encircled the tower and should darkness ever strike them, the gods could respond without delay. They still sat far enough away from each other to allow for plenty of growth, though.

Yeb approached the Great Hall where an elder male emerged with a rickety step and thinning limbs. Dark hair hung around his gaunt face which softened a bit when he smiled.

"Welcome to Arket, god of light," the mortal welcomed him with arms thrown into the air. "I am Kinsen, what brings you to our humble village?"

"I seek a place for my son to grow discreetly," Yeb said in a low voice.

"I see," Kinsen muttered. "I can arrange that. May I be honest with you though?"

"What is it?" the god asked leaning in.

"I hoped you were here about the problems," the elder whispered to him.

"Tell me," Yeb urged, motioning to the hall.

They walked into it together, but the townsfolk already saw the murmurs and knew of what they spoke about. The door shut and Yeb joined the villager in a back room. The weary male sat and pressed the tips of his fingers together while he spoke in strained syllables.

"There is much trouble to be found, my god. People bicker over bartered goods, some rise while others struggle and there is much infighting. There are beatings, one or two killings, and theft, a lot of theft."

"How could such things happen here?" Yeb exclaimed.

"Oh, no, not just here. It happens in all the villages. It is the worst in Taran."

"I will find a way to fix this," the god promised. "First I must return to speak with the others, but when we see you next, we will have a plan."

"Thank you, my lord," the elder said rising from his seat and bowing to Yeb.

The god left Arket with a heaviness. He returned to the tower and went straight to his chambers where Rila snuggled with baby Manuun on the bed.

"Did you find a place for us?" she asked as he entered.

"I found naught but bad news, my lady."

"What do you mean?" She bounced the infant in her arms.

"The people in the villages have been doing wrong to each other. They argue and fight and steal, and sometimes kill."

"How can this be?"

"I do not know, but please let me persuade you to stay here until we have fixed this."

"Of course, I wish for our baby to be safe."

"I will resolve this," Yeb promised, kissing her on the forehead and then planting one on the top of Manuun's.

Then he summoned the other gods to the War Room. Garta and Rica came – she holding Timku in her arms. Teylaan came too – miraculously in full clothing. Yeb explained the situation to them in full.

They stood beside the table, listening intently to the horrors that Yeb relayed to them. Then Garta turned to Teylaan.

"How could you not know of this?" he accused. "You have that ball that allows you to see anything you wish. Surely you knew, yet you said nothing."

"Yes, I saw," Teylaan defended, "But what good is information without the tools with which to use it?"

"What do you mean?" Rica inquired.

"I first noticed when I came across a fallen folk who I did not have scheduled to die. I started to pay closer attention to my orb and saw the crimes that the people committed. I said nothing because I wanted to understand why they would do such things."

"And do you have answers?" Yeb pried.

"I have guesses. One common source of conflict is that the people have no way to consistently barter. Perhaps if we were to provide them with a form of standardized currency, they would not need to argue so over the cost of goods and services. It might resolve many conflicts before they ever begin."

"Rica, you could make beautiful coins for the people to trade right? We could distribute them to the people," Garta speculated.

"I could certainly perform such a thing," she replied

"But that is not all, is it?" the light god concluded.

"No, there is another action I think we must take, one you will like much less. Giving the people less to fight over will reduce their ill-favored deeds, but it will not stop them. Evil festers because there is no punishment for their crimes. There are no laws, and there is no order. There must be rules that they are all required to follow and there should be penalties for failing to obey them."

This suggestion gave the gods pause. They never even considered that they might need to punish the common folk for bad behavior. They felt at loss for how they might go about doing such a thing.

"There ought to be different punishments for different crimes," Garta concluded. "For things like theft, fines should be paid using the coins. For crimes like beating another, offenders should be locked away in cages for a time. For killing another, they will never be allowed to walk free for the rest of their lives. The worst of the criminals shall be kept here until time steals them away."

They all nodded solemnly at this plan. Garta's judgment rang true, but they found it hard to accept. They started with turning one of their middle floors into a dungeon. They placed a wall down the middle of the room's expanse and lined either side with cells. Then they placed cells along the outer, arching walls. The number of cages they created formed a harrowing image for the gods – Rica pulled her infant's face into her bosom. She had no desire to color this place at all, so they left it completely grey. While Yeb and Garta finished forming the barred rooms and creating keys for the locks, Rica created a hoard of coins which she left on the bare floor of another level in the tower. The coins grew so numerous that she needed to create a waist-high wall to keep them from spilling on top of her. Nearly the entire floor hid beneath the mass of treasure. Baby Timku stood leaning on the side of his crib and stared at the shining currency which his mother created before his eyes. She then filled up sacks with it and floated them up to the War Room.

In the meantime, Teylaan set to work on making the system of crime and punishment more organized. After all, much of the decisions made involved the use of time and no one could better flesh out Garta's ideas than Teylaan. He engraved six laws on to three ebony slabs.

Never Steal
Never Kill, unless in self-defense
Never Bear False Witness Against Another in a Public Forum
Do Not Enslave Another
Do Not Beat or Maltreat Another
Always Obey the Will of the Gods

To go with these slabs, Teylaan created giant books to record crimes and criminals that committed them. He even started one for himself so that he too could catalogue all offenders along with their crime and sentencing. He then wrote handbooks for addressing crimes. Those caught stealing something had to pay the worth of whatever they stole or tried to steal and if they could not pay that amount, they spent one year in prison for every hundred coins they failed to pay. Killers spent the rest of their days in prison. Any who gave false testimony during a trial were banned from public forums for the rest of their days and served five years in prison. Any caught keeping a slave would be forced to service the gods in their tower until the end of their days. Any caught beating or maltreating another served between three and twenty years depending on the severity of this crime. Those who defied the gods faced whatever punishment the offended deities wished for them to suffer. Special exceptions could be made to those younger than twenty if the community felt it right and all cases save for those of defiance to the gods were ruled by the general assembly's vote and presided over by designated village leaders. If asked, the gods could come to judge these trials, but only upon request of those already hearing the case.

Teylaan took these things and met the others below in the War Room. He presented his materials to them, but found that their arms were too full with Rica's coin packs to carry anything else. So he flew to Taran with the first set of law documentation and presented them to Sulac along with the coin that the others brought. They explained their currency system to the immortal as well as their plan for a justice system. Sulac grinned widely when they informed him that he needed to step up as a leader in the city and preside over the trials to ensure that justice was served fairly to those who deserved it. He also needed to control the city's treasury and communicate the people's financial needs to the gods. Settlements could gain more money in their treasury by completing milestones and thus progress would always be encouraged. They also urged Sulac to take on some staffing to support his duties during times where he needed to delegate. Throughout the entirety of this mandate, Sulac's spirits soared. He waited for this moment for so long and relished in having all this power bestowed upon him. He nearly died of ecstasy when the gods empowered him to create a force to police the people and investigate criminal activity.

As directed, the immortal ordered a prison be built in the city and he joined the gods in presiding over the first trials where they facilitated over a hundred cases. Many involved simple theft and using the new money system, the courts issued that fines be paid to the victims of these thefts. Yeb and Garta could not help but feel some horror at the more severe crimes. Without law and order formally in place, some tried to take it into their own hands and see their own brand of justice dealt. Folk beat each other half to death and some died over these disputes. While Yeb and Garta felt partially responsible for the circumstances which led to their crimes, they knew they needed to stand firm in supporting the predefined punishments so as to discourage others from repeating these foul deeds. What ultimately encouraged them to persevere through each of these cases was the people's eagerness to see justice dealt. This gave them confidence that crimes such as these would be dealt with in full – that such transgressions no longer went unpunished. When the proceedings finally ended, the town jail neared completion, but could not yet hold the convicted. The gods flew those guilty of murder and assault to the tower and locked them away there. Teylaan made sure to catalogue all of this activity and to make note in a new magic scroll when, if ever, their prisoners needed to be released. Then the gods moved on to Kinam and then Arket to establish the same systems in those settlements.

When they finally finished with this venture, they turned their attentions to the dark forest. Through Teylaan's orb, they saw that it grew in size. Seeing the rapid increase made the gods glad they no longer needed to worry about crime in the villages. Soon enough they would face an evil from the outside and could not afford one that lay within. When Yeb felt that the villages stabilized, he brought Rila and Manuun to Arket where Kinsen ordered a large home built for them. They arrived under the cover of night with only Yeb's light to guide them so as to not draw attention to their arrival.

"When can I see you both again?"

"Whenever you like," Rila answered. "Come by night and stay for the day, then leave at night again. I want no special favors for our son. He must grow like any other boy so that he can become as great a person as his father. A life of pampering will not provide him with this opportunity."

"You have chosen wisely, I will come only as you have said."

"Will you stay tonight?"

"Of course," he assured her with a grin. He stroked the side of the infants face with a finger. "I look forward to seeing him grow." They set the sleeping babe into his new crib and Yeb joined Rila under the covers.

Demigod

The years passed by in a blur. With law and order established, both Arket and Kinam flourished. Soon enough, triplet cities surrounded the god's towers, each with sizeable populations. Garta spent much of his time training soldiers for the inevitable battle against Tubu's forest of darkness. In addition to all of Teylaan's other duties, he checked in on the forest through his globe from time to time. Nothing ever seemed to leave the shrouded borders, but it grew in mass as time went on which made Garta increasingly anxious to launch an attack against it. Rarely did the god of justice and might make a return to the tower and when he did, he spent those precious moments with his growing son. Timku inherited his mother's dark brown hair – which she kept neatly trimmed – as well as her lighter build. Nothing made Garta happier than spending time with his boy, but it was during these moments of bliss that he felt the strongest about marching against the darkness. When it came upon them before, it took so much from them – he would not allow such a thing to happen again. Still he worried. To march into the forest would be of great risk no matter how large the army. The people also no longer remembered the dangers of Tubu's might. Too many generations passed by for them to truly know their enemy.

Teylaan too looked to the future of their world. He felt pleased with his contributions, but knew that they needed far more than a magic globe, a time keeper, some scrolls, and a set of laws. The world grew rapidly and he knew that the gods needed something to help them counteract this. They could fly quickly, yes, but distance proved itself as a great enemy to them during Tubu's assault. Teylaan aimed to defeat such a foe. He spent his days scurrying about his workshop. When he did not care for the dead or record the acts of criminals, he busied himself with inventing a machine, the likes of which even the other gods could never have imagined. He found focus in this work and it helped with his mad ramblings, but other poor habits died a bit harder. Many times did Rica come to check on him only to find that he forgot to wear any clothing. She scolded him for his blinding nakedness, but her chastisements did not make Teylaan remember his garments any better than before. Even worse was when he tried to leave for fragment collection like this.

Tired of his neglect, Rica set to creating something she hoped would solve Teylaan's problem. She created a pair of teeny black shorts out of fabric as stretchy and lightweight as she could summon. She also made him a slick black robe with blue trim which parted and sealed at the middle, making it remarkably easy to slip on and off. It came apart with ease when the wearer wished to remove it, yet remained shut during even the most tumultuous of movements. She presented these gifts to him with a forceful mandate to make use of them. Before he accepted them, he demanded one favor from her. He wished to have the same, light, wiry cords which grew wildly from the top of his head to also grow from his lower jaw, chin, and upper lip. He longed for something to reach for during times of deep contemplation and found that grabbing at the hairs on his head took far more effort than he liked. So Rica granted this to him and he in turn wore the clothing which she made. Teylaan delighted in the small shorts and most of the time forgot he even wore them – Rica took great elation in knowing the time god's private parts would always be somewhat covered. Teylaan made frequent use of the robe as well over time. Since Rica made it so easy to get in and out of, he found changing into it far less of a burden than putting on ordinary garments.

While Garta toiled away in the creation of a legion of light and Teylaan worked on his invention, Yeb took to matters of the present. He made regular visits to each of the city leaders. He trusted the people to uphold the laws and to keep advancing civilization forward, but a part of him still feared what would happen if they left the common folk unattended. The last time the gods departed from them for a time, crime came into being and Yeb had no desire to find out what new evils could emerge from the people so he kept them under close supervision. Travelling around like this not only gave him a chance to steer development, but also an excuse to make more visits to his secret family. Because he became so common a presence among all the cities, no one questioned his stays in Arket, no one, but Sulac.

The immortal had a feeling all along about what kind of "assistance" Yeb required of Rila. Despite all the honors and power bestowed upon him, he still felt the utmost bitterness toward Yeb for flying off with that which he felt belonged to him. In the beginning, it was he and Rila that the gods expected to give birth to a village – he and Rila who shouldered that burden, *together*. He felt the distance increasing between them, of course, but he never thought she would wound him by running off with another and having a child with him – god or not. He vowed to himself that he would find a way to bring ruin to that family, though he still feared moving against Yeb head on. The status that the god so foolishly gave to him would be the means by which Sulac manipulated the people into doing his cruel bidding for him. He did not yet know how he wished to play this, so he started small by planting rumors of Yeb's secret child and his affair with Rila. He created fictions about his paying them special favor and letting them distract him from his duties to the people. Some would have found the story of Yeb's hidden family touching, but it being presented to them as an uncovered secret soured the taste of this tale of love and turned its flavor into something more of a scandal. Once Sulac planted the seeds of this uncouth deception, he merely sat back as the stories and speculation escalated further.

Yeb remained unaware of these insidious murmurings. He lived for moments when he could spend time with Rila and Manuun. The boy grew – not understanding his father's true nature until he reached adolescence. He knew that Yeb had important things to do, but neither Yeb nor Rila ever went into specifics about any of it. In his childhood years, Manuun took great pride in simply knowing that his father had such an active role in helping people, though he still longed for the times when Yeb came back to him. The arrangement became harder as the boy grew older. He saw other little boys and girls out and about with their parents, yet Yeb never came anywhere with him, even during his visits. Then he too caught wind of the rumors which Sulac started. People his age looked upon him differently. Some acted overly polite and gave him whatever he asked of them. Others looked upon him with fear and envy. They walked around him rather than by him – giving him frightened looks the whole way. Even adults treated him differently and either vied for his favor or avoided him altogether. Eventually it all became more than he could bear so one day he confronted his mother

"Who am I?" the boy demanded.

"You are Manuun, my son, of who I am most proud."

"And what else?" he challenged.

"You may be whatever else you wish. I know you will be great at whatever you choose to do." Rila tried to remain patient with the boy, but she had a strong idea of where this led to so she bobbed her head and attempted to leave the sitting room.

"It that because you know I am destined for greatness?" he snarled.

"No one is destined for greatness," she soothed, "it is a choice that we all must make."

"Not even the son of a god?" He raised his voice as she nearly slipped out of the room.

"Why would you ask such a thing?" she snapped – sticking her head back through the room's archway.

"Everyone knows the truth about my father," he whined. "They have always known it, you knew it, father knew it – I was the only one left ignorant to such things."

"Manuun," she cooed, placing a hand around his face.

"No!" He cut her off and snatched up her hand. "Why did he never tell me? Why did he wish it to be a secret and then keep it so poorly? Why did he have me? Why do I not have his power? Is he ashamed of me? Was I a mistake?" Manuun's voice failed after this last question and he fell into his mother's arms.

"You were not a mistake," she said to him softly while she rubbed the back of his head. "Your father and I are nothing but proud of you. He wanted you for no other purpose than to have you as his son and knew very well that you might not inherit anything of his. He and I wished for you to grow up like anyone else. He took great care to make his visits discreet. I do not know how so many others discovered our secret. We would tell you when we thought you old enough, but it seems we should have told you sooner."

"I am so angry," he groaned.

"Speak with your father," she suggested. "Now that you know, we will change things to be however you wish."

Manuun felt betrayed in a way, and fully intended to confront his father now that he had what he wanted from Rila. The mother lamented her child's discovery of the truth as she hoped to keep it from him just a little longer, but that could be done no more. She knew being the child of a god would be a great burden indeed, but Manuun was not the only one who struggled with his divine identity for Timku too suffered from a great inner turmoil.

Rica spent all her days doting over him – smothering him with her affections. He longed to be more than just the child of two gods – he wished to become a respected god in his own right. Yet his mother never so much as let him step foot in the training floor, she never let him see the triplet cities, and rarely even permitted him to leave their dwelling level. One day, during his teen years, the frustrations became too intense for him to bear them quietly any longer.

"Mother, just stop!" He exclaimed while she adjusted the flaring collar of his navy jacket for the third time that day. "No one even sees me except you anyway."

"What is that supposed to mean?" she asked innocently.

"It means I am tired of being stuck on this floor, in this tower. Am I not a god?"

"You're a young god, darling."

"But a god all the same," he protested – taking a couple steps back from his mother and puffing up his small chest. "Are gods not meant for great things? So far all I have accomplished is dressing myself, combing my hair, and cleaning up my room, though you still try to do those things for me as well."

"Well I am sorry I do not wish for you to grow up too fast," she snapped back.

"Just let me start training for something. I cannot just stay in this tower forever."

Then the boy stormed off to upper floors of the tower, not really sure where to go. He possessed the physical capability to leave the tower whenever he wished, but he could never break his mother's wishes. When he finally got to leave the tower, he wanted to do so with her permission and blessing, though it would likely also come with her overbearing guidance. He wandered up the great, spiraling staircase which curled through each floor from the base of the tower up to the upper outlook. Before he reached the top, though, he found himself stopping in Teylaan's lab. He met Teylaan several times and heard a great deal about him – namely his neglectful approach to dressing himself, but he never stepped foot onto this floor before now. He saw Teylaan rushing from table to table creating strange doodads and mechanisms. Timku wanted very badly to go up to the very top of the tower since he also never ventured to that part of his home, but seeing Teylaan scuttle about made him stay at the base of the stairs.

"Timku? Is that you?" He called over, though the boy did not realize the other god noticed him come in.

"Yes, hello, Teylaan."

"My, you have just sprouted up have you not?" Timku's eyes widened at this comment. Not once did Teylaan seem to look up at him, how could he know he grew?

"Yes," Timku replied with some hesitation.

"If your mother sent you, then you can tell her I am fully dressed and behaving well enough." He paused from his work to look at the boy and gesture at his flowing robes with a slight bow. Then he snapped his attentions back to his tinkering.

"No – no that is not why I am here."

"Just going for a stroll then?"

"Sort of," Timku said taking a couple of steps towards Teylaan's workspace.

"You sound a little troubled," Teylaan observed.

"She smothers me," the boy exclaimed. "I cannot go anywhere – do anything. I want to start my path towards greatness, but she thinks me too young. All I want to do is start. I do not need to rush off into anything. I just want to do something other than be doted over."

"I see. How about you come in for a bit?" Teylaan waved the god-child to enter into this laboratory.

Timku walked cautiously into the cluttered space. He noticed the aisles of shelves neatly arranged and covering most of this floor. "What is it you build?"

"I cannot say just yet – do not want to get ahead of myself." Teylaan chuckled vigorously. "I would like to share something else with you though. I think I might have a job for you if you are willing to learn it."

"Yes, please!" Timku shouted. "I will learn anything."

"I am in need of some assistance with my duties to the dead. My work here in the lab is of absolute importance to our future success, I have foreseen this much. The problem is that my duties to the dead leave me with little time for my work here. If someone helped with collecting the shards of the deceased, I should be able to complete this machine before we make our stand against the darkness."

"I can do it," Timku blurted out eagerly.

"Good, let us get you started then," Teylaan announced setting his tools and trinkets down on the workbenches.

They travelled together to Kinam where they came to the home of a recently deceased elderly female. When the pair arrived at her home, they found her family mourning her departure from life. A younger lady opened the door for them and led them to where the rest of the relatives huddled around where the deceased lady's fragments laid in her bed. The gods joined them, some of the folk noticing that a new god stood in their midst. Teylaan handed the boy a vase from the tower. He leaned his head toward the ash, his unkempt yellow hair swinging as he gave the young god a subtle nod. Timku took it from his mentor and stepped to the side of the bed.

"Simply will the matter into the urn and it will do as you command," Teylaan instructed.

Timku looked around the room, not initially realizing an audience would be present for his first performance. He held a shaking hand out and did as Teylaan said. To his surprise, the little bits of matter wiggled out from beneath the blankets and swirled through the air toward him. He made them dance about in a spiraling ball and then sent them into their new home. When he placed the lid over it, Teylaan gave the crowd a low bow and a smile before turning to leave. Timku followed his example, but something stopped him before he stepped through the bedroom doorway. He spun around to face the melancholy group before him. Then he held out the jar in front of him.

"Lay your hands upon Eila one last time friends," he offered. Each came up and placed a hand over the shiny vase. As they did so, Timku continued. "I take her now with me to be among her ancestors and to dwell with the gods, but her memory stays here with you. May you carry on her good works and honor her until it is your turn to come with me."

"What is your name kind god-child?" one of the elder relatives asked in a rickety voice.

"I am Timku, son of Rica and Garta."

"Hail, to Timku," they praised in unison as they placed hands over his shoulders and arms and looked at his youthful face. When they released him, he repeated the bow and left with Teylaan from the home.

"You are a much better reaper than I," Teylaan stated as they took flight.

"I want to keep doing this," the boy admitted.

From Teylaan's workshop, Rica used the orb to watch this scene unfold from beginning to end. When Teylaan and his new apprentice returned to the tower, the boy froze in place at the sight of his mother waiting for them in the laboratory. He did not think of his actions as disobedience at the time, but realized now that this was precisely what they were. She said nothing to him, only rushed over and wrapped him in a firm embrace.

"I was wrong to keep you to myself..." she apologized. "...so wrong!" Then she looked to Teylaan. "Thank you," she whispered.

"The boy has a knack for this work. If he wishes it, I will show him more."

"Yes, please." Timku beamed.

When night fell, Yeb and Manuun sat atop a large, hazel material deposit with their legs dangling over the edge. Yeb let his hands glow freely now that his son knew of his true identity. He flew them to this spot away from prying eyes and listening ears, taking a measure of joy in unveiling his powers to Manuun. But the two sat in cold silence for a time.

Yeb broke the silence first, "I understand why you are angry with me."

"No you do not" the boy whined. "You are never here to understand."

"I knew it would be difficult – to be both a god and a father. I have done my best to act as both."

"Did I not at least deserve to know why you always needed to leave – why you stayed away for extended periods of time?"

"Perhaps you did, but your mother and I thought it best if you grew like any other child."

"Other children have both their parents to guide them. Other children do not have rumors whispered about them, nor do they suffer stares such as I do." Manuun stared off to the dark silhouette of the city. Arket looked so small from here. He found the distance freeing in a way.

"I never wished for you to suffer, my boy."

"I know that – I truly do." Manuun's voice softened.

"What shall we do, now that you know?"

"I want what is impossible to ask of you. I want you to be my father and just my father, but that is not your fate nor is it right for me to request such a thing. What I will ask instead is that you give me space to grow away from your shadow. Let me shed the rumors and the knowing gazes."

"You ask me to leave you alone for a time?"

"Yes I –" Manuun's voice faltered. "If you cannot be there to support me through the pains that your father-ship causes me, then it would be best if you freed me of all of it."

"I am afraid that you will never be entirely free. Whoever spread word of you to others did so in malice and will not stop, but I will grant you what you seek so long as I can be your father once more when you are ready."

"Of course," Manuun groaned as he threw himself into his father's arms. "I just want to become a person that makes you proud."

"I – will always be proud of you, my son, but I wish for your greatness as well. Until I see you next, my boy. If ever you need me, just call and I will hear you."

With this, Yeb carried his son back to his home and then departed. He would not see the boy face to face like this again for several years, though he did check in on him from time to time, from a distance.

Garta built up the armies of the triplet cities to the point of satisfaction. Three grand legions stood ready to move against the enemy remembered only by the gods and immortals. Teylaan reported to the warrior god that the forest grew at an even more alarming rate. Garta pulled Yeb away from his diplomatic duties.

"We can let it grow no larger," he told him. "I am confident that our forces are large enough to destroy the forest once and for all.

"Then let us rally the three armies and march."

Garta bobbed his head and together they flew first to Taran where they met with Sulac. They called the army into service, and found that the Daughters of Rin – now living in a massive rectangular cloister on the back edge of the city – wished to join them. Headed by Matriarch Lira, they came to the gods as soon as they heard of their arrival. Sulac too, insisted on joining them in their recruitment tour. They allowed it with great pleasure – not knowing the scheming immortal's true intentions. They went next to Kinam and then to Arket. This is where Sulac first showed his colors to the gods. As their army marched out of the city to join the combined force, murmurs started about how the son of Yeb did not join them. The gods did not realize that Sulac planted this idea among the people and Yeb did not come prepared to face the calls of the folk for his son's service. When murmurs turned to grumbles and grumbles turned to shouting, Sulac turned his plan into action.

"Yes, Yeb, why does the demigod not join you? Surely we can spare no able-bodied youth from this effort, not even if they are the child of a god."

From his home, Manuun could hear the cries for his service, but his mother forbade him from venturing out. Instead he watched from his window while Yeb came to his defense.

"He is only just old enough to begin his training. He is not skilled in the art of war. Child of a god he may be, but he is one of you. Would you send an unprepared child into combat?"

Despite his pleas, the crowed still roared for the presence of the god-child. Garta stepped forward and called out to them. "Very well, the road is long and he can train on the way, but he will have need of a partner. Sulac, we will need you to join if Yeb's son is to come with us. Is this acceptable to you all?"

The crowd cheered for this. What could be better than having both the demigod and an immortal in their army's ranks? Seeing that the gods outplayed him, Sulac needed to choose between risking his life or his reputation.

"I would be honored," he hissed.

And so they all marched forth to face the darkness. Two gods, a demigod, an immortal, and an army unlike any seen before.

Smokescreen

To Yeb's bitter dismay, the army of Arket joined the Legion of Light with both Sulac and Manuun in its ranks. He felt angry with Garta for allowing such a thing and furious with Sulac for being the one to cause his son so much pain. He hated no one more than himself for not being able to see the treachery hidden beneath Sulac's wide smiles and cheery greetings. Yeb felt as accountable as anyone for what might happen to Manuun in the forest. Little did he care about how upset this turn made the wicked Sulac. The immortal seethed at being outplayed by the enforcer god. He did not think the gods dared to risk his life knowing that he possessed no skill in battle, but perhaps they could be just as spiteful as him. They marched on for nearly a month in order to reach the twisted forest. In order to conserve energy, they only travelled for part of each day and spent the rest honing their skills in preparation for battle. Garta paid special attention to Manuun and Sulac. From the extra weapons that the company carried, Manuun selected a pair of short-swords and Sulac chose a one-handed-sword with a round shield.

The more Yeb watched his boy train with Garta, the less angry he became about the situation. Manuun picked up the art of combat very quickly. In just two weeks, Sulac became a sorry excuse for a sparring partner and Garta realized he needed to set

Manuun up with another warrior in order to continue the boy's improvement. That is when Lira stepped forward to assist the young Demigod. While Garta helped Sulac fumble through his training, the matriarch took Manuun aside to share with him the knowledge of her order. They walked together far beyond the borders of camp with only a handful of the other Daughters there to watch over them. At first Yeb thought to go out as well, but in the end he watched them from a distance.

"We have spent generations in training our unique arts," she explained to him.

She wore light-weight attire with strips of cloth decoratively draped around her shoulders and hips. About her waist hung a thick belt which contained a seemingly endless supply of throwing knives as well as two daggers along with a curled up battle whip. She had her yellow hair tied up in a tight updo, held together by a large, white clip with thin arms that dug into her hair.

"Why me?" Manuun asked. "I thought you only imparted knowledge to other females."

The lady nodded. "Well, you are special to us. It is said that Yeb, your father, was the object of Rin's affections. You are not Rin's child, but you are the son of her beloved and that means a great deal to us. We have no wish to see you die on the field of battle, so we are happy to make an exception to our rule."

Manuun fought the urge to bark at her about not wishing for special treatment, but he knew the knowledge she planned to share with him would surely be of great help in the days ahead and he

knew better than to smack away the hand of friend-
ship that she now extended.

"Then I am honored to receive whatever
knowledge you grace my mind with."

"Let us begin then," she said with a slight
grin.

She taught him the fundamentals of their
unique arts. It started with how they moved. They
embraced the female form and how it curved in elegant ways. They then took this appreciation for their
form and applied it to each swing of a blade, each
throw of a dagger, every crack of a bladed whip. They
even stepped in sweeping motions – keeping a low
center of mass as if in dance. Manuun tried to learn
this style, finding it conducive to his selection of the
twin blades. He learned to twirl his body about and
mix up his swings to constantly manipulate and con-
fuse his opponents. The Daughters of Rin took great
pride in seeing Yeb's son adopt their fighting techniques and quickly match them in skill.

Timku received training too. When not going
into the cities to collect the remains of the dead, he
prepared himself for combat. Teylaan took time
away from his inventing to forge weapons for himself and his apprentice. The time god made a large,
bladed scepter for himself and a pair of sickles for
Timku. They went down to the training floor at every
opportunity and when Teylaan could not take time
to train with him, Rica took her son into the sparring
ring. He learned much from her style of leaping de-
fensively about and striking where the opportunity
presented itself. He had to modify it to fit his use of
the curved blades – adding wide, sweeping strikes,
and radial steps. Teylaan taught him how to make

the most of his reach by fully extending his limbs with each strike and to make use of both his weapons at once.

"The time will come where your work becomes dangerous," Teylaan explained to the boy. "When the battle breaks out, the shards of the fallen will still need collecting and it may be a dangerous task."

"When such a time comes, I will be ready," Timku promised him.

Rica did not look forward to when this day came, but she knew in her heart that Timku would be ready. She took great pride in her son's accomplishments and no longer wished to shelter him from the world. When Garta's army neared the borders of the forest, she, Timku and Teylaan watched from the orb in the inventor's workshop. The soldiers stood lined up in neat rows of brave folk while Yeb and Garta rallied them for the charge.

"This is where we put an end to it!" Yeb exclaimed.

"For too long has the darkness festered in this place – grown like a parasite living off of our lands," Garta continued.

"Only one of you remembers the origin of this evil," Yeb stated, looking to Sulac – the immortal glared back at him. "This means that you do not understand what it is you face. The monsters that live behind this dark veil are cunning, heartless, and extremely lethal. Stay close to your gods and you will see the light once more."

"Who is with us?" Garta bellowed.

"I am with you!" the legion cried out in unison.

The massive force plunged into the swirling black fog to find that the entire forest was filled with it. Yeb's hands poured light around them as he held his boomerangs aloft. He realized that he could not shine enough light to give sight to all of their warriors so he shot forth tiny bubbles of light that bobbed through the air and illuminated the space around them. The soldiers grinned at their god's ability to turn darkness into light, though the smog still danced around them. All remained still until the entirety of the legion entered into the mass of twisted trees. The army plodded through it with Yeb, Garta, Manuun, and Sulac at the center. Behind their line of sight crept lanky creatures like the ones that Garta faced before. They encircled the warriors of the light from behind the swirling blackness. They skipped through the trees and skulked out onto the branches. When the hoard had the intruders surrounded, they leapt into the light and fell upon the gods' army.

Many on the outside of the formation fell to the plummeting beasts, but others thrust their blades up fast enough to slay their attackers. The shadow creatures continued to pour out in an endless flow. Even the strongest of the warriors struggled to keep up with the tireless charge of their enemy. Though the creatures only stood a little taller than the average male, their impossibly long arms and massive, clawed hands tore through those not fast enough to strike back. The Daughters of Rin hurled their throwing knives into the flat foreheads of Tubu's monstrosities. Warriors fired arrows, swung their swords, and held their shields high. Garta threw himself into the fray – demolishing the wiry shadow people with his massive axe. Yeb flew above the warriors to hurl his weapons from a distance. Sulac stayed in the center of the formation, ducking down with his shield held up. The coward's body shook violently as the battle raged on around him. Manuun, however, did not shy away from the fight. He and Lira fought back to back, she wielding her daggers and he his twin swords. When the forces of darkness grew too thick around them and the surrounding warriors fell into ash, Lira knew that she needed to act.

"Get down!" she commanded – sheathing her daggers and withdrawing her whip.

Manuun crouched low and she started to twist the whip through the air. She spun round and round, the bladed tip of the whip slicing through any that tried to rush upon them. Manuun watched as she gracefully twirled with deadly precision. In the chaos, a few of the creatures managed to sail over the cord and land in time to snatch it away from her. Manuun arose to drive his swords through their scrawny chests. Lira took out her daggers again and joined Manuun in felling the monsters. Seeing his son surrounded, Yeb flew to them, tossing his boomerangs around to thin out the mass. When he led Lira and Manuun back to the formation, they realized that the monsters split the army into several small groups in an attempt to divide their strength. Manuun flung himself into the air with an uncommonly high leap and spun his body around with his swords held out to chop down any beasts that tried to swipe him out of the air. When he landed near the separated warriors, he found that his hands now glowed like his fathers. He bathed his allies in light so that they could see better and cut down their relentless enemies.

From the tower, Teylaan arrived at a long considered decision. He could not bear the sight of fallen soldiers any longer and knew that the folk needed as many gods at their side as they could get.

"Come with me," he ordered the mother and son.

He led them into a back room which he carried all of his strange contraptions into. They saw a large machination in the shape of a door with twisting tubes and protruding valves. A series three of brass-colored levers lined a side panel each marked with a different letter – x, y, and z.

"This is the fruit of my many years of labor," he explained.

"What does it do?" Timku asked hopefully as he too grew tired of seeing folk fall to the shadow-spawn.

"It is a way to move matter from one place to the next, he explained. It disassembles what I send through from whatever form it currently resides in and reassembles it at the location I select."

"Why have we not yet used it to aid in the battle then?" Rica demanded.

"Because there is a risk that it may not work. I am as certain of its success as I can be without trying it, but there still lies a small possibility that it will not work. Were a common folk sent through it, they would surely be torn apart, but having studied the differences between Rin's fragments and those of the people at great length, I believe a god could survive such a trip. I do not have time to teach one of you to send me and I would not have asked that one of you try unless I feared the destruction of our forces. None of us could know that Tubu's hoard grew so strong and I did not think it would come to this."

"I will go then," Rica offered.

"NO!" Timku snapped. "You are the only female god in our ranks – we cannot risk your life needlessly. I will go first and if it is safe, you can follow."

"I will not allow my only son to be put at such risk."

"More sons can be born, but a mother lost could well doom our kind. Activate it," the boy commanded turning to Teylaan.

The inventor fired up his machine, pulling the control levers to align with the coordinates he desired. A swirling portal appeared within the bronze archway. Another one opened where Teylaan directed the machine to go. Timku gave his mother a kiss on the cheek.

"See you on the other side?"

"See you there," she huffed.

Timku rushed into the spinning energy and Rica raced back to the globe so that she might see her son come out on the other side. It brought her great relief to see Timku pop into view above the dark forest.

"You are fortunate that worked," she snarled at Teylaan. Then the goddess snatched up her rapier and flew into the machine. Teylaan observed her come out beside Timku. They looked to each other triumphantly and then dove into the hazy canopy.

Manuun's swings left trails of light behind. He leapt between pockets of struggling soldiers and helped them back to the formation. They lost a great many warriors and though plenty of black ash lay strewn across the ground, there seemed to be no end to the dark hoard. Then Rica and Timku burst into the pockets of light and lent their blades toward the effort. They joined Garta first who worked to defend an overwhelmed group of warriors. For the first time since Tubu's attack, Rica and Garta fought side by side. Just like before, Garta provided the muscle while she worked to keep him from getting overwhelmed. This time around, Timku spun about to thin out the enemy forces further. He saw Manuun for the first time since their birth. The son of Yeb struggled to lead a group through the sea of monsters that lay between him and his destination. Timku took flight and glided toward the struggling demigod. He made arching swings at the creatures which stood against Manuun and helped him carve a way to where Yeb provided light and aerial support. They fought in unison– their lightweight, arch-based styles complimenting one another.

Sulac attempted to slink away from the battlefield. He snatched up one of Yeb's light bubbles and searched for an exit to the forest. The coward inched along with his shield held high. He felt as though he made it safely away from the battle when one of Tubu's minions dropped down from a tree and swatted away the immortal's round buckler. Sulac made a weak stab at it only to have the blade smacked out of his hand and his face backhanded. He lay stunned against the ground when the creature grabbed him by the ankle and dragged him off into the darkness. Before being pulled away, Sulac grabbed the light ball. His captor tore him along until he could no longer hear the clamor of battle. Then he felt his foot released and his abductor left him. When he looked up – the light held in front of his squinting eyes – he saw a dense mass of the dark fog spiraling around through the air. It propelled toward him and crashed against the ground where it billowed upward and took the form of a cloaked figure.

"Tubu?" Sulac groaned as he winced past the stray locks of hair that hung over his face.

The betrayer looked a bit different now. His skin no longer had lines over it, nor did it possess the baby blue hue of all living creatures. Now it was dark grey and gave off an onyx steam. He wrapped himself in a black hooded cloak made from thick fabric. The smoke poured out from the opening of the hood and the ends of his long sleeves. The god paced back and forth, his now red eyes glaring at the shaking immortal.

"Sulac," Tubu replied in a sharp, vibrating voice. "It has been many years, has it not?"

Sulac nodded rapidly, pressing his chest up from the ground. His intense fear kept him from giving Tubu any other answer.

"Tell me, ancient one, do you tire of this?" the god continued.

"Tired of what?" Sulac could not hold his voice steady.

"Of the gods," Tubu said in a matter-of-fact tone while he threw his hands up into the air. "Of all the trouble they bring – all the death. The forces of light will win this day, I see that quite clearly, but at what cost? How many good warriors did you watch fall?"

"I – I do not know."

"Precisely! The answer is that you watched too many die and for what?"

"To stop you," Sulac whimpered.

"Stop me? From what? *You* came to *my* home and attacked *me*. I meant no one any harm. Am I not a part of this world? Do I not have as much right to live in it as you – to build up a part of it to my liking? The other gods would deny me this right, they could not accept my differences and they moved to destroy me. That is why I attacked your people before, but I have learned since then. I now know the error of my ways, though the same cannot be said for the others."

"You lie," the immortal barked.

"Do I?" the god challenged. "Think about it, are the gods always altogether just in their dealings. Could you call them fair? Honest? Loyal? In all your years, have they never wronged you? Was it not the gods that put the lives of the folk on a timer – a counter that when empty, steals their life away?"

Tubu's questions gave Sulac pause. The words he spoke had much truth to them and his argument could not be denied. Ever since the first assault, no one saw or heard from the betrayer god. Sulac wondered if what Tubu said about the other gods turning on him contained any truth. And thus the seeds of doubt took root inside of the immortal's mind. Years of feeling jilted and betrayed by the gods left him to sympathize with the shadowy being before him. All his anger and sorrow left him wide open to such suggestions. He would, after all, not be here if not for them. Tubu knew all of this – he could sense the turmoil inside of Sulac and decided to make his final play.

"You do not need them, you know. You are a strong enough leader on your own are you not? Do you really need gods to tell you how to lead *your* people?"

"Of course not," Sulac snapped.

"Well then why are the gods allowed to stay? Why not banish them from this world?"

"How?"

"Tell the people what happened here. Convince them that you do not need to get caught in the middle of the gods' squabble. You can be free of all this fighting – all this death – if you but free yourselves of the gods. In your heart, you know this is true. Good luck with whatever you decide to do, just know that you deserve so much more than this." The god returned to the cloud of darkness and flew off into the forest.

With the aid of Rica and Timku, the gods finally cleared the last of Tubu's monstrosities. The dark fog around them slowly dissipated until natural light poured onto them once more. The solid black branches of the shadowy protrusions shattered into steaming fragments. When the survivors looked around, they saw the countless piles of glittering ash from both their warriors and the shadow-spawn. Seeing everyone's despair for the fallen, Yeb knew he needed to bring light to the group once again.

"Today, we have conquered the darkness!" He cried. "This is a victory that all will speak of throughout the ages!"

Those left standing let out a resounding yell of triumph. Rica and Garta quickly led them away from the scene and back toward the cities. As the company marched away, Sulac slipped into the back of it and worked his way to the middle so as to make it seem as though he never left. Most were far too tired to even notice him rejoin them. Yeb, Manuun, Timku, and Lira stayed behind. The Matriarch knelt beside the fragments of some of her fallen sisters. Timku surveyed the extent of the work that lay before him.

"Timku," Yeb called – waving the boy over.

The god-child glided over to the light bringer. "Yeb, it is good to see you again, it has been many years." In fact, it had been a great many as Yeb had not returned to the tower at all since Timku was small.

"Yes, and you have grown much. I hear you now collect the dead."

"That is right. I have learned a great deal from Teylaan and my mother."

"You are also quite skilled the arts of war. We were fortunate for your aid."

"Very fortunate," Manuun added as he stepped over to them.

"Timku, this is my son, Manuun. You two met as infants, but it has been a long time since then."

"It was a pleasure to fight beside you, Manuun." The boy stated. "You fight with unmatched grace and fluidity."

"I learned from one of the best," Manuun said loud enough for the young matriarch to hear.

Lira looked up to meet Manuun's gaze and gave him a pained smile.

"You should know that the smoking, black ash cannot be collected as it will only burn through any container you try to put it into. Just bury it here beneath the earth," Yeb explained and the boy nodded his head in somber acknowledgement. "Is that how you come to be here with such speed?" Yeb asked looking at the portal above them.

"Yes, that is a result of one of Teylaan's inventions. It teleports from one place to another – so long as the machine runs, the doorway stays open. Teylaan believes it will only work on a god, however. "

"That is unfortunate," Yeb sighed. "Still, Manuun, I would like you to come and see your birthplace if you will fly with me."

"I will, father." Yeb picked Manuun up in his arms and together they flew away.

"You ought to rejoin the legion, my lady," Timku advised the matriarch.

"Could you bring me to them, when you are finished? I wish to remain in the midst of my fallen sisters just a bit longer."

"I would gladly provide such a service."

"Thank you," she said with a bow.

With that Timku flew up into the portal to retrieve a crate of the ornate jars. He made trips back and forth between the battlefield and the workshop to collect the shards and then resupply himself with urns. Though she did not speak the entire time, Lira's company gave some comfort to his work. The process took hours on end, making him glad for the company of at least one living person. When he collected all except for Lira's sisters, the natural darkness of night fell upon them. He then placed the remains of all the fallen Daughters into the vases and returned to the workshop. On his final trip back to the decimated forest, he had Teylaan shut the portal down and he took with him a net. When he returned to Lira, he collected Yeb's floating light bubbles in his snare and carried them down to her. Then he tore holes in the ground and poured the steaming black matter into them where he hoped they would stay buried forever. They spent the night there together in companionable silence and enjoyed the dull glow from the entrapped lights.

Sulac meanwhile, sat in camp with the survivors of the struggle. He wasted no time in inciting bitterness toward the gods. He started with those he deemed the most distraught at the number of losses they suffered and built up from there.

Forsaken

Rica and Garta led the army along at a rapid pace. Whereas last time, they wanted to go slow and be rested for the big battle, this time the folk wished only to get back to their homes as fast as they could. The gods decided they should do a victory tour where they dropped off each city's armies one at a time. The people agreed to this plan, but wanted nothing more than to be as far from the field of death as they could. Without Yeb with them, they found that they needed to stop come nightfall whether they wanted to or not. In several days, Timku and Lira rejoined them – he flying her away from where her sisters fell. She desired solitude so he rejoined his parents at the front of the march. They walked onward as a family.

While the others marched, it took Yeb and Manuun only a couple of days to reach the tower by air. Yeb brought him first to the tower's top to show him the primordial egg. Then he brought him onto Yeb's floor where he and Rila conceived and gave birth to him. He even held onto Manuun's old crib. He led the boy to where he stashed it away inside a thin storage room. Manuun marveled at the exquisite furnishings around him and at the sheer expanse of this dwelling.

"This can be your home too, whenever you want it to be," Yeb offered.

"Is this not a place meant for gods?"

"Gods – and friends of gods –enemies of gods too. It is a far bigger place than you can imagine and there is room for all kinds. Besides, if ever you wanted to become a god, I could make it so. As I saw during the battle, you are already half-god."

"I will think on it," the boy promised. "Perhaps it would be easiest to become all god rather than half god and half ordinary."

"God or demigod, being born the child of the gods is not an easy thing, I see that now and I am sorry for the pains you suffered growing up."

"I know you did not wish it and you could not have known that it would be so. I am glad you had me, glad that I am at least part god. I do have one question though."

"What is it?"

"Who is Sulac? Who is he to challenge the gods like he did when he called for my service? To rally the people to his cause? What makes him so conceited as to run for his life during the battle like a coward? What makes his life so precious and his hatred so strong?"

"These are all good questions, my son. Many of these I do not yet know the answers to. He, like your mother was granted the gift of eternal life and we made him an important member of the folk. I always thought him a strong leader and a good friend. I no longer know who or what he is."

Yeb did not know that the gods would find the answers to these questions much sooner than they hoped. When the legion arrived in Taran for the first victory parade, Sulac ran to his supporters and spun a tale of the god's indifference towards them. He made a point of emphasizing that they did not even find and destroy Tubu. He already had them on his side about Yeb's son and found that inciting outrage over the volume of fallen warriors took very little effort. The procession ended and the celebrations began. Dancers ascended onto a massive stage which the folk built to keep their minds busy while the warriors marched against their enemy. A variety of musicians also entered onto the stage to play instruments which they invented. Some were made to bang on, others to strum and still more made brilliant sounds when whispered into. The thrumming melodies filled the air while dancers in small clothing pranced about the stage – some female, others male. They spun to every whining cord, thrust their limbs to the beating drums, and leapt into each other's arms when the whistling pipes called out in unison. The people around the stage danced merrily with the performers, but not Sulac. Instead, he skulked through the crowd offering phony condolences to families of the fallen while also insinuating that the gods threw their lives away for nothing since Tubu yet lived. By the time that Yeb, Manuun, and Teylaan joined the celebration, over half the city stood ready to forsake their makers. When the performances ended and the gods arose to the stage to make their address, Sulac finally obtained the backing he needed to make his defiant stand against them.

"We have won a great victory," Yeb started with his arms out. "Today we banished evil from this world once more and freed ourselves of the darkness."

"Are we truly free?" Sulac challenged. "Does the head of the alleged monster not still live? Will you not come and plague your people with even more death and destruction than you have already wrought? And for what? The squabbles of gods?"

"ENOUGH!" Garta snarled seeing that Yeb stood stunned by this public assault on the god's intentions.

"You were there in the beginning," Rica added. "You saw what evils Tubu brought into this world."

"I saw a fight between gods which cost the lives of many of our people, nothing more."

"This person is a coward!" Manuun blurted out. "He ran from our fight as though his life was more valuable than anyone else's."

This time, Sulac prepared himself for a challenge to his character. "Yes, I ran," he admitted freely. "Many of us did in seeing the terrible slaughter that our gods – our false protectors led us into. Had I not done so, I would not be here to speak of the horrors that our people suffered because of their selfishness. They think nothing of our lives – they spend them freely."

"How ungrateful can you be?" Yeb snarled. "We gods gave you existence, we gave you laws, and we fought tirelessly for your safety. The common folk are not the only people to lose that which is precious to them. Or do you forget that Tubu took Rin from us? Does she fade from your memory despite her statue standing right before us?" Yeb pointed to where the golden sculpture stood tall above them and the people wavered in their convictions.

Sulac came prepared for this too. "Oh yes, I remember, Yeb. I remember that immediately following this loss, you aimed to replace the missing piece by taking from me what I held most precious."

"Rila had more than enough of your sniveling by then," Yeb shot back. "I stole nothing from you nor did I replace Rin. I simply moved on, a feat you seem incapable of achieving."

"Are you listening to these feeble justifications?" Sulac called out – turning to face the people. "Have they sufficiently answered even a single accusation? They expect us to believe that they want what is best for us. They promise that we can trust them. Friends, I was there when darkness arose and then fell – I joined our forces when we put it down again – and I can tell you that there will be no end to this mindless conflict. The gods use us in a war that has no relevance to our existence. Could we not rule ourselves? Do we not know what is best for our own safety? The gods gave us life and law and taught us a great many things which we should all be eternally grateful for. But they gave us much pain as well. Yeb put your lives on an ever ticking countdown to the end. The gods could make us all as immortals if they wished it, but they chose to give us death instead. No matter what they say, it is because of these so-called protectors that we will never be free from the pains of our own demise."

The gods stood looking out at the crowd from the top of the podium. They could not believe the words that filled their ears. They believed it even less when the crowd roared in thunderous agreement. Lira and her remaining sisters looked on with horror as nearly the entire city denounced their gods – their protectors.

"To forsake us, is to forsake all our help and protection," Garta warned. "Once you have sent us away, we will never return here, no matter how great your need."

"You see, my friends," Sulac hissed. "How conceited of them to think that we cannot defend ourselves! We do not need their so-called protection. No, my gods, I assure you that is no longer needed here. Who agrees with me?"

The crowd cheered out in support of the conniving immortal and the gods dropped their heads in bitter regret of this day. Yeb nodded to his fellow deities and to his son. They all took flight, Manuun carried by Timku. Yeb remained to give his parting words to the people.

"From this day forward, you, the people of Taran, will be free of the gods. We will no longer interfere with your lives. We will not speak to you or come to your aid. It is my sincere hope that you are prepared to live out the rest of your days without us, for we will never again come back to you."

Yeb remembered the day when the gods promised their people that they would never abandon them and his heart grew even heavier. The god crouched low and propelled up into the air. He took one last look down at the mass of people before rocketing toward the tower. He flew through the wide balcony of the War Room where the others waited at the large table – now far fuller than the last time they made use of it. Garta and Rica sat on one side, Timku, Manuun, and Teylaan on the other. Like before, the chair at the head of the table waited for Yeb to fill it. He took the seat, placing his hands over the table and looked to his fellow champions.

"Sulac will not stop at Taran," Yeb pointed out. The others nodded in somber agreement. "We must act quickly if we are to preserve the faith of the other cities."

"We must split up then," Teylaan concluded, "for time is not on our side."

"Agreed, how shall we divide our forces then?" Rica questioned.

"Perhaps it is be best to separate old gods from new gods," Manuun suggested. "Much of Tubu's arguments are against you three, perhaps providing testimony from those new to godhood will sway those who might stand against you. Let us go to my home, Arket. The people there will surely believe me far more than Sulac."

"A wise judgment," Yeb stated. "Are we all in favor?" They nodded unanimously. "Then let us be on our way. Good luck my son," he said, placing a hand on Manuun's shoulder.

The three old gods departed from the tower toward Kinam and the new gods left for Arket through Teylaan's machine. While they spent time deliberating, Sulac already made a move towards converting the other two cities to his cause. Hoping that Yeb made for Arket, he went there himself with a male named Xiru who fought in the battle and felt nothing but spite for the gods. He had large features and promised to act as Sulac's enforcer –concealing a long knife in his jacket for when the immortal gave him the order. They sent runners to inform Clavia and Larun – leaders of Kinam and two of Sulac's biggest supporters – of what transpired in Taran. Both of these traveling parties set forth from Taran the moment the gods left, but did not manage to arrive before the gods at either destination.

In Kinam, Sulac's messengers charged through the city gates just as Yeb, Garta, and Rica landed. Clavia and Larun knew of Sulac's disdain for the gods for a long time and were fully prepared to move against them when he commanded. Upon receiving the message of the folk's victory in Taran, the couple assaulted their gods with spiteful words that rallied the people against them. No matter how many warnings Yeb gave or how earnestly Rica pleaded, nothing could persuade the people when they saw how few warriors walked toward the city. Then came the wails of those who lost someone special on the field of battle. They knew loses were inevitable, but to have so many gone stirred up an anger within the common folk and they drove the gods from their city.

In Arket, Manuun climbed onto the stage built there with Teylaan and Timku by his side. He called upon the townsfolk saying, "People of Arket, I am your neighbor. I am Manuun, son of Yeb and Rila. You knew before I did of my divine birth. I grew here as one of you and though I possess some of my father's power, I will remain one of you until the day that I die." The crowd gathered and looked to him with interest. Around this time, Sulac and Xiru entered into the square. "I am here today because –"

"Because his pathetic father sent him to beg for your sympathy. Because the people of Taran let our gods know that we will tolerate their oppression and manipulation no longer."

"Sulac, what brings a coward like you here? I thought you were more interested in running away from a fight rather than into one," Manuun growled.

"I hardly consider this a fight, dear boy." Sulac felt both a little relieved and a little sad that it was not Yeb who stood here to oppose him.

"Friends and neighbors," Manuun returned to his address. "You must not listen to this stranger. He has only malice toward those who wish to protect him and only cares for his own interests."

Sulac let out a loud cackle. "My boy, I may seem a stranger to you, but I am no stranger to this world nor are you strange to me. People of Arket, this child may be part god, but he is the son of *the* god that brought death upon you – who put your lives on a countdown when he could have allowed us to all live forever. His whore mother is the only other immortal in this world and she sold herself out for the favor and privilege of the gods while I remained faithful to the common folk."

This moved Manuun to leap down from the stage and march toward where Sulac stood in the crowd. The immortal gave Xiru a slight motion of his head and the enforcer departed from his side through the gathered mass. Rila pushed her way between them and turned sharply to Sulac.

"Faithful to the common folk?" She sneered at him. "You have ever only been faithful to yourself. When together, I longed for you to speak of anything other than what we might do to advance our status. It was never enough that we were allowed to keep our immortality – not enough that the gods gave us honored status among the people and looked for us to act as leaders. People of Arket, will you really listen to such a scheming and ungrateful whelp? He speaks ill of the gods, yet he has always wanted to become one."

"My people, have I ever shown evidence of what she says? Any power bestowed on me came from you, the people. The gods left me immortal, yes, but you the people are why I hold any power. My status came from your ancestors and I use it to serve you, their decedents. It would be unwise to give heed to one who cavorts with the gods."

"Enough about my mother!" Manuun screamed. He pushed past Rila and grabbed Sulac by the collar of his long, flaring, green jacket – lifting him up into the air. Sulac dangled helplessly, but knew he had the boy right where he needed him.

"The gods gave me power because they thought me worthy," Teylaan spoke up. "They offered it to Rila as well during her time of being with child and she turned it down in favor of remaining one of you. Sulac has only ever grasped for power, yet in all these years the gods never made him such an offer. Why do you think that might be? I am the god of time and I glimpsed into your future without the gods – it is a path filled only with darkness."

"LIAR!" Sulac howled, still suspended in the air. He noticed the army pouring into the city and grinned widely at Manuun. "Look at those that return from battle. Look how few are left! How long will you tolerate this? Do not be fooled by those who betrayed us in exchange for godly power."

"Be silent!" Manuun shouted, shaking the immortal in the air.

"You see how this half-god thrashes me about so? This is but a fraction of their disregard – their indifference to our kind. The Keeper is not to be trusted. He is but a puppet of those who oppress us. He foolishly traded his life of freedom for an eternity of service to them."

Lira pushed her way through toward where Manuun held Sulac aloft. She followed them there from Taran, but kept her distance for fear that Sulac would notice and put a stop to her interference. Manuun caught sight of her and sent a smile over. She paused for a moment before shouting, "Please brothers and sisters. Do not send away your gods."

"Another slave to their purpose," Sulac cried out. "Tell me, friends, do you wish to hear the testimony of those under the gods' thumb or do you wish to rise up with your brother and show them that we do not deserve their tyranny – that we demand freedom from them! Tell me what have the gods ever given you except for death and heartbreak?"

Disgruntled murmurs rippled throughout the audience and the tide seemed to turn back towards Sulac's side, though not as much as in the other cities. Timku stood frozen in horror at the scene that unfolded before him. Teylaan said all that he felt he had to say on the matter and now tensed himself for whatever action came next. Lira looked despairingly to Manuun who set Sulac down to the ground and gave him a bitter shove. Rila gingerly took her son by the arm. She nearly led him away when Sulac opened his mouth once again, knowing he did not have the city's full support.

"Today we send our gods a message: They gave us death so that is what we now give them." Out from behind a curtain of people, Xiru leapt behind Manuun and stuck his knife through the boy's back and out his chest. Manuun gasped and all around people yelped out in surprise. "If they ever plague us with their manipulative and controlling ways again, we shall bring them even more!"

Timku unsheathed his sickles and Teylaan held his scepter high in the air. Rila let out a mortified scream and Lira fell to her knees. Xiru withdrew the weapon from Manuun's body. The boy winced in agony and began to tear apart into the little polygon's that gave him form. Then the time god smashed the end of his staff against the podium, sending a wave of energy crashing through the crowd. Timku bent low to pounce upon Xiru when he noticed that none of the common folk moved any longer.

"What have you done?" he asked glancing back to the god who worked hard to keep time still.

"We must leave here now. Time is frozen in place around us, now go. Take Manuun and his mother."

Timku did as instructed, taking up Manuun in one arm and Rila in the other. "My brother in arms, I will mourn your passing until the end of days," he whispered into Manuun's ear, hoping that it might still receive sound.

Then he followed Teylaan through the portal and back into the tower. When they entered into his laboratory, Rila came back to animation and fell against the wall beside her while Manuun's body fell apart into ash, which Timku quickly levitated before it could touch the floor. Rila wailed while Teylaan hastened to retrieve a vase from a nearby shelf. When he came back, Timku placed the fragments into it, but looked up to Teylaan with remorse. "He deserves a better one."

"I know," his mentor soothed. "We shall ask your mother to make him one – that is but a temporary resting place."

Timku handed it to Rila who hugged it tightly as she continued to scream. Teylaan shut down his machine. Timku thought to summon the others, but they arrived in the laboratory before he found the need. Yeb looked to them with wide eyes and an open jaw. He dropped to his knees beside Rila and placed his shaking hands on the vase. Rica and Garta stood in silence while Timku threw himself into their arms.

"What are we to do?" Teylaan cut in, though he knew what the response would be.

"WE LEAVE!" Yeb howled. "Not just the cities, but this entire world. We let them have their precious freedom from us and we wait to see just how long it takes for them to perish. They cast us off and I forsake them in return. May the darkness take them!" The last words came from a failing voice and the other gods heeded this command without debate.

Garta, Rica, Timku, and Teylaan flew around the outside of the tower and descended to its base. There they used their mastery of matter to raise the entire structure straight up into the air. The folk watched as the gods carried it farther and farther away from where it once stood. Many, like Lira screamed for the gods to come back, but Sulac took care to ruin any chance of that happening. The gods lifted their home until they could no longer look upon the ground. Then they constructed a wide platform where they set it down. This is where the tower sat until the end of days.

Rise of the Common Folk

The scene in Arket became more explosive than Sulac ever could have imagined – the sudden disappearance of the gods and then the subsequent departure of the entire tower making it all that much more dramatic. Sulac knew the gods would likely still be watching from above, but to have their tower entirely removed from sight made this all seem quite a bit sweeter. In order to ease the chaos of these events, Sulac reminded the residents of Arket that their elder, Malari served as their leader all these years and that she would continue to do as much without any intervention by the gods. He knew the elderly lady was well liked and that she could restore order with little effort – he chose this place for his attack for this very reason. He hoped to put an end to Yeb, but his son worked just as well, perhaps even better.

"When it all evens out here, meet me in Taran," he told her. "Take Luretan with you if you like."

"I will join you there when the people are calm," she promised and then the immortal departed with Xiru by his side.

As Sulac and his enforcer travelled back to Taran, Xiru asked, "Was it right – what I did? Killing the son of the god like that?"

"Do you feel guilty about it?" Sulac inquired, fully expecting the enforcer to have some regrets about how it all happened.

"No, I just – It all happened very fast and –"

"You are welcome to speak openly with me," Sulac consoled. "Today was a hard day – a painful day. But you did what needed to be done. We cannot advance ourselves if the gods always look over our shoulders and drag us off on their selfish crusades. We have tolerated their rule for all these generations because we feared them and now it is time for them to fear us. You did a cruel thing, yes, but believe me when I say that even this cruelty does not match that which the gods inflicted on our kind. Those memories are my burden to bear and I alone can promise that what you did could not have been done any better. Thanks to you, a new era is upon us. It is an era of kings and queens, not of gods."

"Then I am happy that my hand that allowed this to be so," Xiru said. "Thank you, Sulac."

"Oh no, my friend. It is I who must thank you and I will, just give me time and you will be raised up to a place of honor very soon."

And so the two continued on merrily, but up in the tower of the gods, a far bleaker event unfolded. The gods stood together in Teylaan's messy workshop. Rica made a series of special golden urns, hoping to only ever see one of them actually used. She presented it to the waiting group where Rila held the copper-colored jar. Timku stepped between them and nodded for Rila to open the lid. She took it off and he levitated Manuun's fragments from on vase to the other where Rica sealed the golden container. Then they took it into a small room where

Rica used lighter blues and shinier silvers to color it. In the middle of the room stood the pedestal that Rin's urn sat on. During the time that Rica took to make the new urns, Garta constructed an identical pillar and set it a few steps behind for Manuun's ashes. Rica handed the jar to Yeb for him to place his son's remains in the confined room. Then they shut the door and dispersed throughout the tower, though Timku remained in Teylaan's workshop.

Back in Taran, Sulac and Xiru entertained Clavia and Larun until the arrival of Malari and her son, Luretan. When the leaders finally convened, Sulac welcomed them warmly into his home, but then jumped right into matters of business.

"This city, ladies and gentlemen, is where our revolt began. This is where we first stood up and said 'no more' to our gods. But it would have meant nothing if not for your unrelenting support. Especially in the face of adversity," he added turning to Malari who graciously bowed her head. "What I am about to suggest now is a bit unorthodox, but these are unusual times in which we live. I say that we establish a new way to govern the masses and retain order. Each of our cities already possesses strong leadership, does it not?"

"Indeed they do," Clavia asserted, pushing out her bosom and thrusting her chin high into the air.

"Why not expand this leadership so that we are no longer the conduits between gods and people. We need to become rulers in our own right. Each of us is now responsible for establishing and maintaining a line of nobility. Our decedents will take over for us in our stead. So Malari, when you pass on, it will be Luretan that assumes your place, unless you appoint another. It will then be him that takes on direct rule of Arket and whatever female becomes his partner will be second in command. But the same will be true for females too. Should Luretan have a daughter as his eldest, she would be the default successor to his rule and any male that bonds with her will be her second. If deemed appropriate, a younger child may be made heir, but by tradition it will always be the eldest that is looked to for leadership. This way we can ensure that the directions of our cities will move in a consistent path. It would far better than if the people have to elect new leaders every so often."

"And what is our direction to be?" Malari cut in.

"We grow," Sulac stated simply. "Our sole purpose – aside from maintaining law and order – should be to always expand our cities. Then we must see to the construction of new settlements. We must also build up our arts and culture. Seeing the musicians and dancers during Taran's celebrations made me realize that this is an important part of our civilizations that must also be grown. Armies and police forces are still important. We will just be using them for *our* purposes rather than the gods'. Oh yes, and we will need to change one of the laws – it is each city's rulers that must be obeyed without question rather than the gods and when personally wronged by one of the people, it is us that will get to decide their punishment."

They all agreed that this plan felt correct. So they departed for a time to set it into motion. They all started by expanding the city halls into large palace-like mansions to symbolize the shift in power from god to royalty. No one put up much resistance to this change, mostly because they knew nothing they said could bring the gods back and they needed strong leadership in their absence. The remaining Daughters of Rin retreated into their cloister where they returned to their studies and tried to shut out the pains of recent events. They wanted nothing to do with this godless world, but they also lacked the strength in numbers to challenge Sulac's initiatives. They instead watched as the people turned Taran's City Hall into a monstrous home for a person with even more mammoth ego.

In the tower, each of the gods faced the reality of their situation and each found a different way to cope. Yeb and Rila took it the hardest. They retreated onto Yeb's floor where no one saw or heard from them for a long while. Rila wished to mourn her son's passing in absolute solitude. Wanting her company, but respecting this wish, Yeb moved her into one of the empty rooms on his level. He made a bed and some furnishings for her and moved her clothwork equipment and materials into it. She shut herself in and crafted herself a long, black gown with a matching veil. She felt it right to wear such a garb and so she remained dressed like this for the duration of her solitude. Yeb too fell into himself. He had no desire to look upon the world again or to so much as leave his floor.

Garta and Rica, found comfort in one another. They insisted that Timku stay with them on their floor more often. They felt that everyone needed to be together during this time of sadness and Timku agreed, though he still spent most of his time with Teylaan in the laboratory. Timku felt that he still had a duty to the folk so he and Teylaan devised a plan to sneak into the villages under the cover of night. This might mean leaving remains there for nearly an entire day before collecting them, but it seemed a better alternative than not coming for them at all. Teylaan visited Yeb in his chambers and beseeched him to create several lanterns for the gods to use. Yeb, glad for a task to keep him busy, accepted this request and made five simple lantern cases in which he placed dense cylinders of light. Teylaan sent Timku through his machine into the cities – the boy using the lanterns to navigate into the homes of the fallen. He wore a flaring jacket, tight pants, and calf-high boots with a long swath of cloth draped behind each of his shoulders, all in an onyx hue. To his surprise, he found many families waiting for him. They did not question why he made them wait, but were simply glad to see him arrive.

"The gods may have been banished from this world, but I will not abandon you so long as I yet live," Timku promised them. "Keep faithful to me and I will collect the remains of your loved ones."

The people still regarded Timku as a friend to the common folk. He did not invent death, but merely served as the reaper of it. His black attire became an iconic part of his persona. Some artists even took to depicting him as having a set of dark wings since the twin capes that flowed behind him gave off the appearance of him having wispy rear limbs. Many of the gods became the subjects of stories and paintings. Not all of the people delighted in their exile and still more regretted that they played a part in their removal. They honored their deities in this way in hopes of preserving their memory should they ever return. For generations to come, Timku remained the most prominently portrayed god since he alone still held a connection with the folk. While Teylaan and his apprentice-turned-partner continued their work, Garta and Rica struggled with a decision of their own.

"We ought to have another child," Rica suggested placing her hands over Garta's chest.

"I am proud of our son, Rica, but would it really make sense to bring another god into being? What place for them is there? What place is there for us?"

"Our place may be gone, but our duties remain." Rica looked up to him intently. "Tubu yet lives and is surely prowling about as we speak. There will come a day when we must descend to rescue any that remained faithful to us. Timku tells me of how many are still loyal. If they are still faithful by the time Tubu brings his darkness upon them once more, then we must go to bring them to us. By the time that day comes, the forces of evil will be very strong, so we must be strong as well. "

"I see your point," Garta admitted. "Let us have more children then. We will raise and train them for our final stand against Tubu's forces." And so the couple accompanied each other to the bed to expand their divine family.

When a year passed, the leaders of the triplet cities reconvened in Taran. They found that they could indeed do a perfectly fine job of building their civilization without the guidance of the gods. That is not to say that all went off without a hitch, however. The three leaders struggled with one inescapable truth – they could not be as omnipresent as the gods. They needed to walk wherever they went and could only do so much at a given moment. So they arrived at the conclusion that they needed to appoint those below them to manage tasks that they themselves did not have time for. They planned to build up these courts and take responsibility for overseeing them as well as appoint new people to fill empty seats. They needed people to handle finances, others to uphold the law, and still more to supervise construction plans. They all agreed that there could be no other way to continue growth, but still did not understand to what end they should be aiming for. Sulac assisted them with this. The way he saw it, they ought to ultimately assemble a brand new ring of cities – one with twice the number of locations as the current circle. This would be difficult to do in their current state however. They needed a faster way to travel between two points. They needed innovation and invention. They needed power. So they returned to their home cities and put this next phase into action.

The best thinkers from each of the cities set to finding a source of energy with which to fuel any machinations they might invent. They searched the land for anything that they might obtain energy from, but found nothing. Then one researcher thought to look up. She saw Solan, the great light and realized that it not only gave them light, but also heat. If that energy could be captured and stored, they would have their source of power. So Tiralu, the researcher, worked with her colleagues to find a material that could store and release Solan's energy. They discovered that lighter-colored materials were of no use to this effort so they stuck to dark, absorbent panels and connected them to batteries which they insulated with light materials so as to keep the energy trapped inside the cell. After years of development, they finally found a way to harness power and now they need only develop machines that could make use of it.

During this time of research and development, Rica gave birth to twin siblings after a particularly violent pregnancy. The primordial egg came through for her once again and she emerged with a baby boy in one arm and a baby girl in the other. They named the boy Shirun and the girl Shira. Both babies had their father's build right from birth, which explained Rica's agonized outbursts in full. What could not be explained were Rica's repeated visions of a city that lay beyond the swirling energy of the egg – she could not figure out why a city would lie within the egg or if it even truly existed. She, like Teylaan, opted to keep this vision to herself for the time being.

Garta took great delight in seeing his new children and in that moment believed that they made the right choice in having them. Timku took what time he could to play with his infant siblings. Nothing brought him greater joy than to have the babes in his arms and he finally understood why his mother experienced such hardship with letting him go. Not all would stay whole in the family however as Rica arrived at a somber conclusion.

"It will be my turn to leave you to raise our children," she said to Garta one day.

"What do you mean," he asked bewildered.

"Though Teylaan watches from his globe and Timku continues his work as reaper, we gods need to be more involved in the world. The folk are enjoying a time of great growth, but soon enough I fear that Tubu will strike. I feel that I must be there myself, but in disguise so no one can recognize me. When a generation has passed, no one except for Sulac will remember my face anyway."

"But why go back to them so soon? They made it clear that we are not wanted."

Rica bowed her head in thought before looking back up and responding, "There is something that feels off about it all. Tubu's forest, Sulac's revolt, our banishment – it all just feels far too perfectly arranged to not bring me concern. Is it not odd that we never once saw Tubu in that forest? What if that was but a distraction he constructed for us, a grand trick."

"The last time Tubu made his play, he did nothing quite as subtle as what you suggest," Garta argued.

"Yes, but think, my love. Many years passed with no sign of him save for his growing forest. What could he have done in that dark chasm by himself if not scheme against us? What is to say he did not walk among our people under disguise like he did before? He knew he could not construct a force to take us on like he did before, but does it not seem like the folk have been manipulated to turn against us once more?"

"So you think this is the same scenario as his first act of betrayal?"

"I think it is but a slower plan of attack. I feel it is one that must be studied from the inside."

"Very well," Garta conceded. "Go and live among the people once they recognize you no longer.

I will care for the growth of our children while you examine our enemy's involvement. But promise me you will not take on more than you can manage."

"You have my word," she promised – leaning her face up to plant a kiss on his.

With a source of power available to them, the common folk discovered ways to create their own lights. They also learned to make doors slide open by merely touching a button and how to make a wheeled vehicle propel forward using a light-powered engine. They constructed two types of clunky carts: one with a roofed wagon to hold up to four passengers and one with an open topped back to load materials into and transport elsewhere. Both types had a seat in front where a driver pushed and pulled various levers and cranks to control the speed and direction of the transportation devices. With the use of these inventions, the common folk transformed their cities into magnificent metropolises, redoing many of the buildings to make use of their updated technology. They also used materials with darker, cooler colors like blacks and dark greys to construct their taller buildings. Homes became apartment complexes, jails became enormous prisons, and the mansions turned into miniature fortresses of luxury and wealth. They built roads between the three cities and before even a single generation passed, the rulers of the triplet cities felt ready to move on with the next phase of their plan. Civilization progressed faster than Sulac ever could have hoped for. The common folk did more than rise, they ascended.

The Court of Darkness

Time slipped by as the common folk raced toward their goals for expansion and self-improvement. Before establishing the six new cities, the three rulers decided to construct a large tower where the home of the gods used to be. This would be a place where all the rulers met to discuss progress, obstacles, and solutions to any problems that arose. The tower stood only a fraction of the height as the one that once rested there. They kept a staff in it to maintain the facility and fix any power issues, but by and large the tower did not get used unless the council needed to convene. In this tower, on the tenth and topmost floor of it is where Sulac met with the decedents of his original colleagues – an elderly Luretan as well as Lirarun, the son of Clavia and Larun's eldest daughter. Luretan brought along his fully grown daughter – his wife already being passed and Lirarun, a young bachelor, came alone. Sulac brought with him his first companion since Rila, a young woman named Yira with whom he planned to start a family. Though he needed no heirs, a part of him always wanted to start another family since any children he ever had with Rila were long since passed. They sat at a table built for more than eighteen attendees and Sulac began the discussion.

"We are here to address an unforeseen obstacle to our progress," he started. "We are now in a place where we are able to create an entirely new ring of cities twice the size of what exists currently. The only obstacle? Money."

The other leaders nodded in agreement. "The financial disparity in Arket is already quite drastic between the wealthy and poor," Luretan added. "I can hardly fund my own city let alone one or two more."

"Yes," Sulac hummed. "The situation is the same amongst all of us. That is why I present to you all, a young entrepreneur named Taben who thinks he can solve this problem by reinventing the money system we currently have in place." He then nodded to Yira who arose and opened the doors to the chamber and revealed the young male.

Taben sauntered in. He wore a finely tailored, shimmering suit and arranged his cropped hair neatly atop his head. He dropped a case down upon the table and looked up to the council bright-eyed. No one, not even Sulac recognized that this spunky young businessman was truly Tubu in disguise. He found a way to shift his entire form so as avoid recognition by even those who knew him. He flipped open his case and withdrew a shard of abyssal material which seemed to have energy swirling within its semi-transparent surface. To the council it appeared but a normal rock. Only Tubu understood what power it held.

"This is something I like to call Darkstone," the young folk announced. "It can be found below the ground where the great battle between light and dark once took place. When initially buried, this substance was an extremely volatile and unstable material, but years beneath the ground fused it into something beautiful, something of great worth. It is one of the rarest materials found across the land, but not as rare as the coin of the gods."

"So," Luretan chimed in, "you propose that we make new coins from this dark substance?"

"Not quite," Taben/Tubu corrected with a grin. "My proposal is this. You mine the material and measure its weight. Then you use that amount to determine how many credits you possess."

"Credits?" Sulac inquired.

"Yes, credits. They will come in the form of thin sheets made of common materials that on their own have no worth, but thanks to being backed by the Darkstone, can now have value."

"And there would be enough of this Darkstone to fund the wealth of nine cities?" Luretan clarified.

"Oh yes, that and more if you wished it," Taben beamed.

Out of lack of a stronger plan and an eagerness to continue expansion, the council commissioned a rapid mining of the Darkstone fields – stashing the substance in their tower. Little did they know what affect such a currency had on the people's greed. The folk would covet credits, not knowing about the wicked substance that drove their lust for more. The council knew the stone's evil origins, yet could not see that darkness still lived within it. The precious stone filled the treasury of the tower in the shape of uniformly carved blocks. The three leaders each took a little of it to store in their own treasury and made sure that one did not get more than the other. Then they arranged for the creation of thin, black chips which would be distributed in place of the coins and named them credits just as Taben suggested to them. Then they hosted a massive currency exchange where each citizen could replace their coins for an equal number of credits. Some tried to hang on to the old currency, but found they could no longer do that when people stopped accepting it. When the lengthy process concluded, the council finally possessed the necessary means to continue their civilization.

The leaders did not distribute the credits out equally because they wanted there to remain a large population of poor people. They needed folk to feel eager to move on to new lands where they might find better fortune so they left them in destitution for a time until they announced to the world their plans for creating a second ring with six brand new cities. Those who suffered lives of poverty applauded this decision and readily volunteered to contribute their talents toward the effort. Before ground broke on the project, the council selected six new members, promising them each a share of the Darkstone bank. They also provided entire fleets of carts including a new type of transportation machine. Inventors designed a long type of cart with eight wheels and two compartments attached by a hitch with a driver seat in the front. Such vehicles allowed up to twenty of the folk to cram onto the benches within and ride to a location far away. Those making the trip packed themselves in without complaint. Their eagerness for a new life even dulled the unpleasantness of their bumpy ride.

And so civilization webbed outward. The six new cities sprung to life without much delay. By the time Rica decided to make her return to the world, she could no longer recognize it through Teylaan's globe. He also showed her that civilization did not grow alone. The great chasm that Tubu originally fled into also expanded. It seemed to devour the matter around it – pulling it into its foggy abyss. Though this progressed slowly, it still gave the gods much to worry about. Rica dressed herself in a long, hooded cloak of a dark green hue. She wore a dull purple shirt with ruffled sleeves and grey pleated pants with black heeled boots that came up to her ankles. She followed Timku through Teylaan's device and arrived with him in Taran. She felt the city was large enough where she need not worry about Sulac ever noticing her presence there.

"Where to first mother? It is unwise to linger near me for long," he advised.

"Show me to where the Daughters of Rin stay these days."

Timku frowned. "Very well, they could certainly use a visit from their goddess."

"Has misfortune befallen them?"

"Not exactly. We've watched the world change much through Teylaan's orb, but there are many things missed when not examining the world from – well from the world. The Daughters have found that life is difficult for a group which is publicly loyal to the gods. They needed to go into hiding to avoid being destroyed and the last time I saw them, it seemed like they could really use some inspiration – some hope."

Timku led his mother through the narrow alleyways until they came to the main strip. He stayed behind the shadows of the alley and pointed Rica to a large building which thundered with music. She bowed to her son who she could no longer consider a boy and departed toward her destination. The streets bustled in a way that she never could have imagined. Sun-carts buzzed by in either direction and folk hastened past buildings on both sides of the street. She followed a line of people into the enormous building which had colorful lights shining out of it. The glowing sign on the top read: THE SWANKY PLUME. She stepped inside and felt the blaring sound crash against her. She saw a glittering golden interior with legions of tables spread out on two floors. A stage took up most of the back wall where young ladies danced in sequined small-clothes and waved thick, feathering plumes around in the air. Rica wondered how this could possibly be where the Daughters of Rin hid. Did her son point her in the wrong direction? Did she somehow misinterpret his instructions? Then she looked around a little more carefully and noticed all the women of different ages serving tables, performing, and attending to guests. The dancers wore their slinky uniforms and the servers had their own. They wore teeny skirts and tight long sleeve shirts that dipped low and left much of their breasts to be seen. Was this what the Daughters came to?

"May I seat you Ma'am?" The hostess asked when she returned to the front end from seating other guests.

"I —" the goddess still looked with distress upon the scene. "I am looking for a daughter," she concluded.

"Oh, does she work with us?"

"Yes, I think so."

"Well I know all the girls on our staff so if you tell me her name I can go find her for you," the girl folded her hands on top of the tilted table and waited patiently for the disguised goddess to start making sense.

"What? Oh no any of them will do."

"Are you saying that you have more than one daughter here?" The light-haired hostess leaned over her podium to get a better look at the guest.

"They are my friend's daughters and I do not know their names, I just want to find them. I am sorry if this all seems strange to you, it is just – well I have been away from these parts for a long time and it is all so strange to me."

The hostess's eyes widened. She looked around and popped out from behind her podium to take Rica by the arm. "I am sorry my lady," she started. "I think I understand now, let me get you to a seat alright?"

"Yes, thank you dear."

Rica allowed the girl to lead her up a set of stairs to a third level of the establishment. While the second consisted of a wide floor jutting out from the wall and held up by supports, the third only contained balconies which sat a good distance away from one another. The hostess brought her into one of these and sat her down in a booth meant for six.

"Someone will be with you in a little while," the girl announced. "Please just be patient while I find the person you are looking for."

Rica nodded and the girl left. After some time in solitude, two new ladies, and older one dressed in the server uniform and one younger who wore a dancer's garb came to join the goddess. They shut the balcony curtain and gave Rica a bow before joining her in the booth.

"You came looking for daughters," the older one began.

"Yes," Rica said in a wavering voice.

"Well, you have found us, Lady Rica. I am Olbia and this is my daughter, Selestia."

"It is a pleasure to meet you both," Rica replied in a quivering voice.

"It troubles you to see us like this?"

"It has just been a very long time," Rica confessed.

"Yes," Olbia conceded. "Much has changed since the last time you saw this city. I hope your judgment does not befall our order," the elder female said looking to the stage performance.

"No!" Rica exclaimed. "I mean how could I pass judgment? We have been gone and you remained. It is a joy to see you still intact. My true sorrow comes not from my disappointment in what you did to survive. It is just different. I watched from afar as the cities changed, but to be here with the people again makes it seem as though I never really saw a thing."

"It has been difficult – for us," Olbia allowed. "We stood against Sulac a little too firmly and he ordered that we disband or pay the price. So we did, but in secrecy, the Daughters never really ceased to exist. We arose once more, but this time, we needed a cover – private cloisters would no longer do. At least those are the stories I know."

"But you are safe here?"

"Oh yes, we chose this profession wisely. We keep our training grounds in the basement where we spend our days and toil away here at night. Even if Sulac knows we are here, there is nothing he could do that would not rouse the outrage of the people. We are the premier entertainment establishment in Taran – this security comes with a price, but one we gladly pay for the preservation of our beliefs. I must admit to you that our faith is waning after generations of waiting to hear from the gods but fearing none save for Timku would ever return."

"Then I must say something to all of you."

"It will be hours until our customers leave," Olbia lamented.

"A few hours are nothing to a goddess," she consoled. "Return to your duties, I will wait."

And wait the goddess did until every customer took their leave of the place. Then Olbia and Selestia gathered the other Daughters around the stage. Rica glided down slowly to them, allowing them to see her for her true self immediately. When she landed, she turned to address them.

"Daughters of Rin, faithful handmaidens of the gods, I come to you with an important message. We gods were banished from this world by the common folk's demand and so we departed from it. But even in our exile, we keep watch over you all, and we are very proud of those that remain faithful to us despite the odds. I want you all to know that we still fight the darkness and when the time comes, we will charge into battle with you once more."

The ladies let out a resounding cry of jubilation and kept the goddess as their honored guest for a time.

As years passed, the council of the nine cities grew stronger and the outer ring flourished. Though much building could still be done, the leaders turned their attentions to other matters. Tubu once again found a way to influence their decisions by killing one of the rulers named Manan and taking on his appearance. In this way he entered the council and suggested new policies which would provide them with better control over the often unruly populace. He argued for a closer relationship with the entertainment and news industries so that they may be able to influence the kinds of messages that their people received. Furthermore, ever since the invention of ray-gun technology, crime rose to new heights and Manan correlated this to the widespread use of these weapons. Sulac, however, argued that this technology could not be blamed for the reported increase. He attributed it instead to the rapid growth in the population. He also asserted that these weapons were in fact not owned on as wide a scale as Manan claimed. Being the products of experimental technology they could only hold a few charges at a time and burnt out if fired off repeatedly. They also only came in a bulky rifle or heavy pistol style which made them an inconvenient accessory to criminal activity. Others initially felt the same way, but Manan had them under his charms and so the council fell onto his side of the argument – except for Sulac who did not fall for the young spitfire's persuasive techniques.

The immortal became increasingly desperate. He saw himself as a champion for the people's freedom and to have such things suggested and widely accepted among the council brought great fear to him. He stood in passionate opposition to any of these plans until Manan/Tubu realized that Sulac no longer served as a useful puppet. His stature posed a significant threat to Manan's ability to move forward with his plans since he knew he could never have the full support of the council with Sulac so vigorously against his ideas. After a particularly volatile session, the disguised Tubu summoned a young male named Zenran to his chambers. The large folk served as the bodyguard to Sulac and descended from Xiru's line. Tubu knew the ambitions that lay dormant within the youth's heart and preyed upon them without reserve.

"Zenran, thank you for joining me," he greeted.

"To what do I owe the honor, Councilman?" the bodyguard replied stiffly.

"Relax, my friend. Do you not tire of always being at attention – always being in service to another – does your family not deserve more than to be the loyal bodyguards of an ancient being?"

"I am honored to serve Lord Sulac," Zenran replied hastily.

"Please, Zenran, drop the charade. Your family has served Sulac for too long. There is much this world owes him thanks for, but his outdated thinking is now standing in the way of important legislature. The people need more than guidance – they need a level of control asserted on them. Without it, they will continue to do harm to each other and themselves."

"What are you proposing?" Zenran demanded.

"I propose we solve two problems with a single act. I have been in talks with a group of religious zealots for a long time – under an alias of course. I am acting as their benefactor and happen to know they will jump at the opportunity to put an end to the one who has been with us since the start of time."

"You mean to kill Sulac?"

"Yes, my friend. Killing him not only removes the sole opposition to plans for advancing society, but also shows how projectile weapons are a danger to leave in the hands of the common rabble. AND it will make public to the world that fanatic god worship is a danger to us all. When it is done, I will step in and arrange a marriage between you and Sulac's eldest daughter. Since Sulac, in his arrogance, has made no plans for his succession, the children will need help in moving forward and will be very susceptible to my suggestion."

"What of Sulac's wife?"

"Oh, she must die as well – it must be alongside her husband though, otherwise suspicion will arise."

"This is a lot to ask of me, Councilor."

"There is far more to be gained by you than lost. Keep in mind, you need not pull the trigger, only supply my pawns with the weapons and point them in the right direction. Doing so benefits both yourself and every other mortal being in this world. And if you refuse, there are others that would reap the rewards of this deed."

"What if I went to tell my master of this plot?"

"You could certainly complicate my plans by doing that, but given his political stance against me, any unproven accusations would hardly be heard and believed by many. This is your one chance for greatness, son, take it or be gone."

Zenran paused for a moment before announcing, "I will do as you say."

When the delegation from Taran returned home, Zenran departed from the palace to receive Manan's delivery of ray-guns and strange ball-shaped explosives. He delivered these to where the fanatics stayed. When he arrived, he got a strange feeling about the lot of them. They seemed more like hardened mercenaries than jilted religious whack-jobs. They armed themselves too naturally and showed no signs of nervousness or hesitation when Zenran dictated the plan. He ignored these signs given that he already got himself in too deep.

The pack of alleged fanatics waited at the crossroads of two major streets. They hid in dark carts parked along the sidewalks until Sulac and his wife came upon it while on their way to an extravagant ball for the rich and powerful citizens of Taran. When their cart and escort arrived and turned onto the street where the assassins hid, they leapt out from their carts and threw the circular bombs to the middle of the three royal carts just like Zenran instructed. The grenade released its violent energy into the car, decimating it and its passengers into millions of square fragments. Passengers in the escort vehicles, including Zenran, piled out and opened fire on their attackers who shot back as they made their escape. The aftermath of the attack left remains of the rulers indistinguishable from those of the cart. For the first time in centuries, Timku appeared publicly in daylight so that he could extract the correct fragments and help the people clean such a mess. Rica looked on protectively in case any should try to do him harm as well. When the streets were cleaned and the assailants caught, the city held a grand ceremony in honor of their immortal leader whose death caused them a great deal of distress.

Neither Timku nor Rica stayed for the procession, but instead left through Teylaan's portal and arrived back in the workshop. The Keeper cataloged the jars for Yira and the cart's driver, but they left Sulac's vase on one of Teylaan's workbenches, unsure of what they really wanted to do with it. They delayed their judgment for a time to watch events in Taran unfold.

"One of the folk is not behind this," Teylaan announced.

"What do you mean?" Rica asked in shock at his certainty.

"Had this been the scheming of a common folk, I would have been able to see it unfold. Furthermore, even if I simply missed it, I am able to look back in time at past events and I still cannot find the source of this destruction. Only one such as us could cause this. Even now, I cannot see what happens in the house of Sulac. Tubu is there."

"Then I must return," Rica concluded. "Timku, alert me when more is found out, I will work on getting close to this."

"Be safe mother," Timku warned.

Teylaan fired up the portal for her and she departed from them. What the god of time could not see was Tubu arriving in the royal house of Taran as Manan with Zenran by his side. He came to Sulac's children as a caring friend of their father and promised to help them restore strength to their rule. As promised, he suggested to the eldest daughter, Salma, that she take on their former bodyguard as her husband to rule in her stead and keep her and her younger brothers safe. She felt too distraught to see any other alternative. Sulac never imagined Taran without his rule and never prepared for his own death. Neither Salma nor her brothers ever received any leadership training. None of the children planned for such a day and two out of the three took no issue with their beloved protector assuming rule of their city. Salma married Zenran right away with the youngest child, Rimj looking on gleefully. The middle child, Keeran, did not buy into any of it. He suspected that his parent's death had more to it and vowed to investigate the matter. Tubu, meanwhile now possessed a council devoted entirely to his cause. He finished building his court of darkness.

A World Without Gods

Once Tubu's shroud lifted from the Palace of Taran, Timku and Teylaan could gaze into it. They discovered what Tubu set into motion and picked up on the troubled Keeran who immediately set himself to uncovering the truth about his parents' mysterious deaths. It all felt too convenient for him to have his parents die and then see their former bodyguard so readily assume the throne for them. He being only twelve years of age grew up the day evil took his parents from him. The gods watched as he snuck out of the palace and visited the place of the attack. He went there over and over, hoping to find some clue that brought him proof of what he already suspected. Seeing an unlikely ally in the boy, Timku set off to tell his mother of the inquisitive child.

In another part of the tower, Garta played and trained with his twin children. They lived happily together and looked forward to what precious moments they had with Rica when she returned to them from the world. Living less happily was Yeb who wasted away in his private quarters. All this time, he never so much as left his room. Sometimes he did not even move from his bed. This all changed when Rila emerged for the first time since she moved into her living space. Yeb jumped up off of the bed and ran over to embrace her. He almost forgot she lived there – forgot that anything other than his pain existed. Now here she stood before him, just as lovely as when he last saw her. But she had a serious look about her and purpose filled her eyes.

"I am done making pretty things." She announced. "I wish to move on with my life."

"Do you mean to say that you want another child?"

"No, that I have no wish of."

"But it has been many years, surely you are now rested and ready to –"

"Enough, Yeb!" She barked. "I wish to do more for this world than just bear children that are fated to die whether by old age or the tip of a blade. I wish to see if you are still willing to make me into a goddess. I turned away this offer before because I saw no need for me to have it. Now I realize that all the common folk are my children and in a world without the gods, they are surely suffering. Make me a goddess so that I might go down and have the power to better their existence. I promise I will be subtle and use those gifts with care. I wish only to move about with haste and to give the people the hope that they deserve."

"You are a far better creature than I," Yeb said flatly. "Come with me, I will grant you precisely what you ask so that you can go to our people – something I do not yet have the will to do myself."

With the change in Taran leadership, Tubu – under the guise of Manan – held a meeting of the council. Without Sulac's opposition, he found it quite easy to sway them into agreeing with his plans. They decreed that blasters and explosives could no longer be owned by the common folk. Sulac's death proved to all the people that ordinary citizens could only misuse those instruments of death and that they had no practical need of them in a civilization which now enjoyed uninterrupted peace. Only those in the police force and military were permitted to have such weapons at their disposal. They also voted to place heavier restrictions on what entertainers and reporters could present to their audiences. Manan commissioned a group of researchers to look into a means by which images and sound could be broadcast for the masses to view from their homes and in public establishments. They also motioned for greater funds to be put into the advancement of projectile and transportation technologies. Manan held his most dubious of plans for another grand assembly thinking it better to revel in this small victory.

When little Keeran could not find what he looked for at the scene of the crime, he turned to the city archives. He scoured the shelves for historical and religious texts. The boy found plenty of books, but none contained any depth or substance to them. Little beyond the most meager of myths about the gods could be located. Those that did exist were written in language fit only for very small children. He wondered how this could be, since Timku's continued presence in the world served as proof that they indeed existed in more than just bedtime stories. The historical texts made no mention of the gods at all nor did they say much about how the original three royal families came to power. They recorded little more than the progress of the nine cities from the village of Taran to the world that they now knew. He slapped his hands down on the table in bitterness, wondering where else he could possibly go to find out anything of interest to him. That is when Rica approached under the disguise of a librarian.

"Are you finding everything okay?"

"I can't find out anything I want to know!" he burst out.

"Shhh," she warned. "I think I know what section you want go to for that topic."

Before he could protest that she didn't know what subject he wanted to learn more about, she proceeded toward an aisle in the back of the building. He arose and followed, to find her waiting with a folded-up piece of parchment in her hand.

"Here you are," she chirped, handing him the letter and strolling off.

He unfolded the paper to see her message. It contained an address to a clothing shop just a bit down the road along with instructions to ask the person at the counter for something to lighten his spirits and tell them that he came by the instruction of Rica. The child did as the note advised and arrived at one of the secret headquarters of Taran's Seekers of Light – an underground order of those who remained faithful to the gods and prepared themselves for their return. The clerk at the counter could not believe his ears when the son of Sulac spoke the secret entrance code. He doubted the child's interest and his claims that Rica sent him, but he had no desire to argue with him while customers walked around. He led Keeran into the basement where two of the other members discussed recent matters of weapons control and artistic censorship. They met the boy with as much shock as their gatekeeper, but welcomed him in and heard out his story. They decided that despite his being the descendant of their fiercest persecutor, he fit in perfectly with them and they shared with him all the truths that he desired.

Eventually Zenran caught on to the boy's constant disappearances from the palace. He knew of the child's suspicions over his parents' death and knew he might become a threat in time. The ruler could not publicly take care of this issue so he employed the tactics he learned from Manan and sought out lower class, struggling individuals. The king paid them to drag the mischievous boy down an alley and kill him, but to make it look like a robbery gone wrong. They would all serve ten to fifteen years since the murder would look unintentional and no motive could be found for premeditated assassination. Zenran promised that riches would await them when they got out. They accepted the offer and followed Keeran toward the Seeker's hideout. When the opportunity arose, they rushed upon him and tore him down into the shadowy space between two tall buildings. One pressed him up against the wall and covered the child's mouth. The other two muggers closed in, one drawing a dagger. Before they could execute the deed, Rica entered the alley entrance.

"What sort of coward preys upon a child?" she called down to them.

"Leave us, whore! Find a new alley."

"Big mistake," she growled, withdrawing her rapier from beneath her shining green cloak.

The muggers panicked at the sight of such a blade, though they did not recognize it as the weapon of a goddess. She rushed upon them, the train of her cloak flapping about behind her. The one with the knife rushed out to meet her while the other two froze in place. Rica pounced into the air and sailed above her attacker. She landed behind where he missed his swing and flipped her sword so that she held it backwards – then plunged it into the thug's back and ripped it out. His body crumbled to ash behind her while she twirled her blade back in front of her. Without hesitation, she plunged the tip of the sword into the remaining thugs. Keeran fell to his knees – now in full belief that this mysterious lady was indeed the goddess she claimed to be.

"Thank you," he gasped.

"They are not the last that will try to try to end your investigation into the truth," she explained reaching a hand down. "If you become a knight for me and stand against the darkness, I will be your guardian."

"Okay," the boy said jerking his head up and down.

Then a portal popped open beside them and Timku sprung out with three empty urns in his arms. He set each down on the ground and put the lids down beside them. Then he pulled the ash of his mother's foes into the vases. He capped them and scooped them up in his arms again. Timku bowed to the both of them and ran back into the portal which closed behind him. When he returned to the laboratory, he saw that Rila stood there with Teylaan. The young god could sense the power emanating from her body.

"I aim to do as Rica does and lend aid to the folk – my kin."

"I think I know where you can start," Timku said with a bow of his head. He walked over to the orb and summoned images of the various Seekers of Light hideouts scattered throughout nine cities. "My mother turns her attentions to securing a new ally," he explained, "But our current allies could use our aid as well. Go to them and let them know they are not alone. Help them wherever they are in need of it. Tubu is bringing darkness into the world but this time it comes from within and our people will need a light to guide them through it."

"Then that is what I shall be," Rila promised.

"Follow me, my lady," Teylaan instructed. "When you are ready to come back, call upon me and I will open a doorway for you to return."

He sent her through the machine and into the hideout of her first destination. Thus began her mission of visiting the members of their underground faithful. They came from all walks of life and had varying degrees of belief in the gods. What they all shared in common was a distrust of the new laws and impositions that their rulers placed upon them. They saw the early signs of the disease that Tubu spread throughout the civilization and intended to fight it with or without the gods at their side. Rila went from hideout to hideout, finding several located in each city. She reinvigorated their faith in the gods as well as their hopes that they did not face Tubu alone. She found purpose in making these tours and discovered that she possessed a godly power to disappear from sight when she wished it. This made it easy to intercept any that meant to do her people harm. She spent little time on the streets, preferring to phase to the tower and then back to wherever Teylaan had her go. Garta crafted a spear for her since she could not very well take on enemies of the light without a weapon. She had little need to conceal it since she could just turn it invisible even if she herself wished to remain seen.

While Rila and Rica served as champions of the people, Tubu set into motion the rest of his plans. Posing as a much older Manan, he called for a meeting of the grand council. The deceiver congratulated their work with making the civilization a safer place for the folk to live. He then introduced the next phase of stabilizing their society; this part would take a bit longer. Manan proposed that the population could not continue to grow for much longer. Even with the small bit of Darkstone reserves in the tower treasury, they would eventually run out of the substance which backed their currency. This meant they eventually needed to stop printing out credits. The population had to be capped, but there could be good news to this. In order to keep numbers at the desired level, they needed to put an end to birth and an end to death. They could usher in a new era where in exchange for one's right to reproduce, eternal life would be granted. With the right algorithms and a properly constructed machine, they could institute what he called the Legacy System. Rather than let people's ashes be taken to the heavens where they just sat in bottles for all eternity, these fragments should be used to reconstruct deceased folk. In this way everyone could be reborn again and again and never have to worry about death.

They needed to plant the idea first and then, when the dream became a reality, most of the people would be ready. Step one involved collecting those that died between now and then to test the machine and usher in the first reconstructed folk – showing everyone what miracles could be performed. Not everyone would be on board with the idea, but if they played this right, enough might enroll in the program to obtain their desired effect. Then he explained the second element to this process. Collecting their own ashes made the last god obsolete and finally freed the folk of his lingering presence, but that would not be enough. Any texts or images that made reference to their existence needed to be destroyed. Furthermore any words that harkened back to the age of gods should be removed from the language. This second part unnerved the council a little, but by this point rumors spread about what truly happened to bring about Sulac's demise and Zenrans' ascent to power. None dared to speak out against Manan and despite their suspicions they remained blind to the leader's true identity. As the years went on, pieces of the plan started to fall into place.

Rica guided Keeran through his teen years and together they worked to uncover the subtle changes that Tubu made to the world. The boy took notice that artwork which once represented gods no longer hung anywhere and that even the childhood fables could no longer be found in the archives. All references, names, and even words relating to the time of the gods now became vigorously discouraged like profanity. Not even Rin's statue stood in the center of Taran any longer. The pair realized that these were the changes that led to the world's destruction. Unless one looked at the signs from the perspective of the larger picture, they could not be identified, but when examined in unison, those with eyes that cared to look could easily see that the decisions of their leaders set their inevitable undoing into motion. Rica guided the boy along a path of fighting to expose the wicked plot that lay beneath their noses. If anyone stood a shot at swaying the minds of the people, surely it would be the son of their beloved Sulac.

Timku came to the realization that he had not aged in all of these years. He retained his looks as a young adult with no signs of developing any further. He found this a pleasing consequence of being the descendent of a god and could not help but wonder if this would have been Manuun's fate as well. He became so busy with caring for the dead and dying that he never gave much thought to his immortality as his mind constantly focused on the lives of mortal beings. To his great dismay, however, this eternal mission – his life's work –came to a devastating end. He returned to Teylaan's workshop after five separate trips to homes of the allegedly dead to find that nothing waited there for him. He let the number of these consecutive occurrences reach five since he hesitated to question the god that he still considered his mentor. After the fifth time, however, he confronted the Keeper about this miscommunication.

"Teylaan, I need a word," the boy called out when he returned through the machine.

"It has troubled me also, my boy. Five times I sent you with an urn and five times has it returned empty."

"That is because when I arrive there is nothing there to collect."

"Indeed," Teylaan hummed while stroking his scraggly beard.

"What is happening?"

"They are taking them."

"Someone is taking the shards?"

"The common folk are collecting their own. It is royal decree that all dead be collected by the proper officials. It seems they too know how to count down till the end of a person's days. But how? Wait, yes, they do not count – no – there are too many. It is their machine."

"What machine?"

"The one that counts – that computes – it beeps when someone is ready – flashes their name across the screen. It is marvelous – also diabolical – I want one."

"It must be like their other inventions that run off of the light that Solan shines upon them."

"Yes, the stuff courses beneath their cities, fuels everything. My inventions are different – run off something else."

"What does this all mean Teylaan?" Timku interrupted.

"It means they now officially need us no longer, it means that they are banishing the last of their gods. But not the faithful, no, they are hiding the stuff, hoping you will still come. You must continue. I will make new lists – better lists – when one is ready, you must make haste."

"You can peer into the future, what is it they do this for?"

"Something horrible, my boy – something entirely wicked – something that will seal the world's fate. Tubu wishes for a world without gods. He knows this is impossible, but as long as he gets close enough – he still wins."

"We won't let that happen," Timku affirmed.

The Legacy System

Rica continued to guide Keeran, now a full grown gentleman. Together they used his lineage to vie for the attentions of political figures – though most who saw him held lower offices. His fame bought him audiences with judges, town clerks, and even advisors to rulers across the nine cities. They all heard him, but none listened. He tried to play every angle, he reached out to every contact, but no one gave heed to the messages that he brought. No matter how many points he made, the leaders could not connect them. Soon he lost any political clout he had due to his ancestry and found himself branded as a mindless rabble-rouser and enemy to progress. Zenran went to great lengths to paint him as such even before Keeran's rally for the people's attentions began. The ruler continued to spread malicious witness against his wife's brother until the final hours of his life. This left Salma to rule for a time since she was the rightful heir to the city from the beginning and eventually her son would take over for her. The only encouragement Keeran ever had came from the validation of having his life always under attack. If not for Rica, a vast number of assassins might have killed him by now.

One group had enough gall to attempt to murder him within a courthouse that just turned him away. They came dressed as officers of the law and trailed them down the shimmering hallways.

When they felt confident that no one could see or hear them, they launched their attack. Then Rica sprung to life and whipped out her blade from beneath her flowing, pink trench coat. The assassins laughed at her as she stood in front of them with but a sword while they held guns. They found amusement in her appearance – a seemingly delicate female wearing a pink jacket, white pants, blue high heels, silver makeup, and neatly arranged hair.

"Get out of the way bitch," they ordered with a chuckle. "We're only getting paid for the one kill, don't make us work overtime."

Before offering any kind of acknowledgement, she twirled through the air and lopped off both of their heads. Her dismembered enemies crumbled apart onto the floor while she struck an unscathed pose – her head held high. "You are the bitch!" She sneered. She did not like the word. It felt cruel, demeaning, and filled with wickedness. But for folk such as these, she used it without regret. Despite her living down among the people for most of Keeran's life, she never ceased to feel as though she could not recognize the world. The laws, culture, beliefs, and now even the language changed.

Eventually, those that wanted Keeran dead accepted the fact that he received supernatural protection, though not all of his enemies understood exactly what that meant – Zenran certainly did not. When the attacks stopped coming and his contacts no longer tolerated his presence and alleged fear mongering, he no longer knew what to live for. Knowing Keeran's distress and pain, Rica decided to push him in a new direction.

"You tried harder than any other," she consoled him as he plopped down on the steps to yet another courthouse that refused to see him. She placed a hand on his shoulder and caressed it softly. "It seems Tubu's influence spread too quickly. We could not have known the people would be so willing to believe him. He did it with such ease. There is only one thing left for us to do."

"What could we possibly do now?" he moped. "No one will listen!"

"No one of power will listen," she corrected. "There are many others who will hear your message and you must gather them to yourself. You need not be the only knight who fights for the gods."

"How?" he asked, his head snapping up.

"Let me bring you to a certain establishment in Taran. I think there are some ladies there who might be able to advise you."

In the tower, Timku's work slowed down. He tried to collect those whose families called for the gods the very second their loved ones passed. To the gods' horror, they saw officers kill any who tried to circumvent the Law of Collection. By rescuing one dead male or female from the council's grip, they condemned each of their remaining kin. And so Timku stopped collecting the remains altogether.

"Go to your family," Teylaan suggested. "I will look to the workshop for a while. Your siblings are surely grown by now, spend a little time getting to know them, you have earned that much. If my predictions are correct, the end will come before long."

Just as the last words slipped from his tongue, the jar containing Sulac's remains – which they left on the same table for years – started to melt from the inside out. Molten goo poured out and started to incinerate the table on which it once rested. The fragments steamed like the black pieces of Tubu's minions.

"Catch them Timku!" Teylaan shouted. Timku pulled the pieces up into the air with his mind while the time god scurried through the aisles. "Help!" he cried out again and then came a ripple through the workshop that held the burning black polygons suspended in time before they could pour out onto the shelves.

Timku and his mentor gathered them all and brought them to the inventor's machine. Teylaan created a portal above the gaping chasm and they tossed the steaming bits through.

"So Tubu can claim any that serve his purpose," Timku sighed. There is no saving them if they have already chosen his side.

"And if he claims them now, that means he prepares to claim the rest," Teylaan added. "Go back to your family, I will clean the mess."

Timku did as instructed and Teylaan set about to repairing the damage to his mortuary. Though most of the urns remained perfectly unharmed, far too many of them burst into flaming globs for his comfort. The loss of his charges rattled him beyond words. While he normally mumbled during work, he now found nothing to ramble about.

Tubu's plan came to full fruition as the decades passed. Television programs now streamed to every household. Reporters provided viewers with the stories that the council wanted told. Singers wrote songs about life that never ended and being reborn into a new body and loving life in the cities.

They sung about sex without babies and living free from the responsibilities of family life. Screenplays brought these fantasies to the screens of homes and theaters. Authors and poets spun tales such as these using words that the council deemed appropriate and palatable for ordinary citizens. Any who rebelled in any way or simply refused to conform to the rules set in place suffered from "accidents" so that they no longer posed a danger.

Using the advice of Matriarch Selestia, Keeran gathered a force of eager young males and sent along young ladies to his new friend. He amassed a small, but faithful and well-trained force. They travelled from city to city at first until finally settling in one of the outer metropolises called Wakan. They bought a factory there and set to the craft of constructing finely crafted light-bikes during the day and using the underground storehouse to train after business hours. They raised an impressive sum of funds which they used to purchase illegal weapons and supplies. Their brand became one of the most prestigious names in the biking industry – Knight Riders. As their order grew in strength and their leader's years came to a close, they finally gave themselves a name, The Keeran Knights. For now they only used the title among their own so as to avoid being discovered. Upon Keeran's death, they made an oath to continue their mission and to be ready when the gods finally needed their forces.

Timku spent time training with his siblings who both grew to rival the size of their father. They also chose weapons of equal power. Shira wielded a mighty war-hammer while Shirun swung a pair of battle-axes. They knew nothing of the world beyond the tower, yet Garta made sure they would be ready to face it when the time came. Timku found that he needed to move quickly in order to properly compete with them. He also discovered that he possessed the ability to blink a short distance away from wherever he currently stood. This proved to be a welcome competitive edge during training and promised to provide a lethal advantage when the real fight came. During one of these sessions, Teylaan barged onto the training floor. Timku froze, knowing very well how little the inventor cared to travel away from his laboratory.

"I have something you must see," he exclaimed before scuttling back toward his own floor.

The family followed him back and huddled around his globe. He displayed images of Tubu's final piece to his puzzle...The Legacy Machine. For the first time, it fired up in full production. Workers poured the ashes of dead folk into it. A conveyor belt dragged them along through the sputtering machination and recompiled the bits into newborns which came out the other side. Nurses scooped up the babes and brought them to the nurseries. On the networks, this grand unveiling was presented as a miracle and an answer to all that the folk ever hoped for. To the gods, it marked the beginning of the end. The rulers announced that in order to gain eternal life, all that the citizens needed to do is surrender their ability to replicate by undergoing a series of treatments to reconfigure their functionality. They explained that this requirement only ensured that the population did not explode out of control and people reasoned that if everyone would just be reborn in the end, then why even bother to have

children or families? Their parts would still work after all, they simply could not produce a child any
longer. This is what the songs and stories, movies
and dramas made them think and dream about. This
grand invention seemed like the end to death, but as
Tubu knew, it only primed them for the reaping. The
betrayer no longer walked amongst them, but instead watched from a distance – his role as Manan
died nearly as soon as all the parts were firmly set
into motion.

On one of her trips back to Teylaan's workshop, Rila heard of the incident with the jars of the
remains. The goddess made sure to visit all of the
Seeker hideouts to warn them not to fall for the Legacy System's lofty promises. They needed to
continue to reproduce normally otherwise the gods
could not guarantee their salvation. Rica delivered
this same message to the Daughters of Rin and the
Keeran Knights. Then she spent the rest of her free
days preparing alongside her family for the coming
battle.

The first round of the reconstructed folk grew
without any of the body modifications applied to
them since Tubu needed them to choose to accept
them. To his delight, people traded in their fertility
readily in exchange for the chance to be reborn.
What they did not know was that they would be reborn with this ability inherently missing from their
bodies. After several generations of this, the rulers
even recommended the use of pulsation repressors
to keep the populace pleasant, though not necessarily happy. Pockets of the faithful found ways to
preserve themselves. Rila helped the Daughters and
the Knights come up with an arrangement to match

three males and three females every five years. They kept these couples hidden so they could raise a family in secret and the orders never had to worry about going extinct.

While society fell into a dull, droning version of existence, a fire lit within Yeb's mind. He heard of all that transpired from Teylaan who paid him longer and increasingly frequent visits. The light god heard of Tubu's victories and knew the end came upon them with blinding speed, yet he felt no compulsion to leave his chambers. The gods warned the folk of what would happen. Did they not deserve the destruction that would soon befall their kind? The more Yeb justified his omission, the more he started to wonder if the people had not already paid their price. His convictions softened at the thought that some small pockets remained faithful across the generations and he finally left his place of exile to summon all of his kind to the War Room. Teylaan, Rica and Garta with all three of their children came, and even Rila took leave of the world to join their council. As always, they left the head of the table for Yeb and sat eagerly while they waited for him to start.

"Soon our people will fall to the great deceiver." *Our people* – the gods relished in hearing Yeb call the folk that once again. He continued, "If we are to save those who never faltered in their faithfulness to us, then we will need a champion down there with them – one that Tubu will not be able to detect until it is too late. I want to send my son down to them – send him through that machine."

The gods leapt back in their seats and looked to their leader wide-eyed. "He is right," Teylaan spoke up. "We gods can do only so much without drawing Tubu's notice, but Manuun could operate on our behalf and give our people a head start. Tubu would not be able to detect him, nor would he even expect his involvement."

"Precisely," Yeb proclaimed.

"Give them a head start to where exactly?" Garta chimed in.

"We return the tower to its former resting ground," Rila concluded leaning over the table.

"We could get them into the tower, but then what?" Garta argued.

"We might bring them through the egg," Rica added. Both Rila and Teylaan nodded in agreement.

"What would that do?" Garta asked, puzzled at the notion. "What goes in always comes out."

"Maybe not," Rica corrected. "When I went through it, I saw glimpses of another world – one where nothing but warmth and a shimmering city of gold could be found. Bright light flooded the space, but not so bright that it hurt my eyes. The images did not hold, they were blurry, and much of my memory of my stay there left me as soon as I returned to you."

"And the both of you experienced this same thing?" Garta further inquired looking to Rila and Teylaan who bowed their heads in acknowledgement.

"Then the rest of you come up with a plan to get our people into this tower, Rica and I will speak with the voice on this matter," Garta concluded.

"What of Rin?" Rila spoke up before they all departed.

Yeb shook his head. "We run too great a risk of Tubu noticing that. It would be best if we sent her ash through the egg with the folk."

Rila nodded and they split off as advised to set their plans into action. Teylaan opened a portal into The Legacy Factory for Yeb to step through. He came bearing the urn which held Manuun. He emptied its contents into the machine and then retreated back through the portal before he could be seen.

Teylaan and Timku analyzed how to retrieve those remains which did not enter into the machine. They found that each city possessed a necropolis where remains of those who did not give into Tubu's plans were kept. In order to rescue them, Timku would need to enter into each and collect the crude bottles. They needed to wait for the right moment however. Doing so now would bring about Tubu's notice and ruin any chance they had at retrieving the rest. Timku vowed not to leave a single one of them behind.

Rica and Garta called upon the voice asking "Great one, what lies beyond this swirling portal or of yours?"

"You already know the answer to what you ask," it thundered back.

"Yes, but how do we get there – permanently?" Rica persisted.

"I hoped you would never need to," the voice admitted. "I always wished that this existence could be your paradise, but I suppose this is just the way of things. The world of which you speak is the place from which you came. Perhaps you should indeed return to it now that darkness threatens to consume the one in which you now live."

"So we have failed then?" Garta groaned.

"No, the people failed, but you will save those wise enough to remain true to the light. My energy will be a doorway henceforth and any that enter shall be transported to the world that came before the world. They will go to Digitarum – their final dwelling place. No evil can exist there, only warmth and kindness – love and light."

"So we can begin sending our faithful through now, and when the end of days come, we can escape with the rest?" the goddess confirmed.

"This is the wisest plan that there can be, it will be your task to save as many as you can." the voice assured her before leaving them once more.

They brought this news to Teylaan and Timku who immediately started sending the folk that they kept stored on their shelves through the egg. Rica meanwhile took Garta and the twins back to the training floor where they readied themselves to lead the charge. Teylaan made a second globe so that Yeb could keep watch over his son. The light god knew it would be years until he could speak with the boy, he knew the child would go through the pains of living in a loveless world, but he also knew that this child could bring about the salvation of all things good which persisted in spite of everything that stood against them. Tubu remained ignorant of Yeb's scheming. In his arrogance, the deceiver did not think the other gods had it in them to stop what he would soon unleash.

Birthright

Yeb watched as Manuun came through the other side of the Legacy Machine. The infant looked exactly the same as when Rila first delivered him, but this baby could not entirely be considered Manuun. It looked like him, yes, and came to share many similarities with him, but he would also be different in a lot of ways. These differences started with his name. When the nurses – dressed in all white skirts and pointy caps – scooped him off the conveyor belt, they did not know who the babe used to be. They carried him into the sterile, white nursery where they put a tag upon his crib with the name KENTU on it. Yeb found it hard to see any differences at first since by all rights this newborn was his son, Manuun. But over time, the god realized that Kentu and Manuun were, in fact, not the same. His son still remained dead, but Kentu could be a new son - a twin born many years after his brother. The god discovered that this simple truth served as the very foundation of the Legacy System's grand lie. No one could truly be reborn using this device. It only recycled their pieces into something new – those that died remained eternally dead.

Yeb watched as the nurses administered the treatments which sterilized the children and made it so that feelings could not bog down their spirits. Though most came out of the machine infertile, the council decreed that all infants still receive the treatments just to be sure. Yeb worried that these re-configuration protocols could affect his son. What would they do to a half-god? The light bringer had to wait to find this out and for the moment, he merely watched as the infant grew under the care of those without emotions or even much intelligent thought. The nurses and doctors buzzed around in a mechan-ical way, always caring for the newborns, but never showing them any affection. Over time, it seemed like this had an adverse effect on Kentu's growth. The babe wailed for attention, but the nurses did not understand his affliction – they possessed no knowledge of his feelings. Then some started to talk of his possibly having a defect and they discussed trying to start over with him. Yeb found relief in knowing that his son possessed an immunity to their treatments, but he panicked at the idea of the doc-tors putting him down.

So Yeb waited until night when the caregivers turned the lights in the nursery off and left the in-fants to sleep in their cribs. Kentu still cried out, disturbing the tranquility of his counterparts. Teylaan sent the father-god into the quiet room. He snuck through the aisles of black cribs and leaned over the railing to his son's. The god let his hands give off a soft glow and poked the giggling child. He tickled and made faces at the love-deprived baby boy. He lifted him out of the crib and walked quietly around the nursery while he lightly bounced his son up and down in his arms. Baby Kentu fell asleep like this and when morning came each day, the nurses found the child calmer and calmer so they set aside their plans to kill him. The god visited his son like this every night, though he knew he would only be able to do this for so long.

Eventually, Kentu grew into a large enough baby to be transferred to the toddler wing. The nurses there put the children through an aggressive program of learning to walk and talk. Here, Yeb saw his son suffer again from the level of indifference which his caretakers showed towards him. Though Yeb knew this would be far more dangerous territory than before, he slipped onto this new floor of the nursery and comforted the boy at night. He kept quiet and no longer allowed his hands to glow for fear of another child seeing him and making a disturbance. He spent nights like this with his boy for as long as he could, but as the child started to formulate words, he knew these visits could not continue. Soon the nurses moved Kentu again to another floor of the enormous child development center. This facility along with the Storehouse in which the massive machine rested could be found in the rebuilt Ebuk. When the children could no longer be considered infants, they transported them away to schools in the nine cities where they continued their development. Like other children, the time eventually came for this to happen to Kentu. They loaded him onto an aircraft with other youngsters his age and sent him to one of the outer cities – one called Litso. The years that followed this change were the ones that brought Yeb the most suffering.

The children shivered when they arrived in the chilly school. No longer did their caregivers leave them in little boy shorts or girl onesies, they now clothed them in teal shirts and pants for the boys and a pink set for the girls. They trimmed their hair and kept it neat. Their instructors demanded that they walk with their backs straight and their heads held upright. In a short time they had the children reading, writing, and counting. During all this time, Yeb watched the child grow from afar. He could no longer make his nightly visits since he feared the boy might tell someone out of not understanding Yeb's identity – or his own for that matter. Any time Kentu acted up, his instructors scolded him and tried to give him more of the treatment, which still had no effect on him. That is when Rila intervened.

At night, she came just as Yeb used to and spent the nights stroking her son's hair and snuggling with him while he slept. She remained entirely invisible while there in bed with him and never woke her son from his slumber. She worried that these acts of affection would not be enough to foster his growth, but over time it seemed like they satisfied his need for love. The doctors believed the treatments did their work and allowed Kentu to continue his development without interruption. Rila remained his unseen companion through his childhood, but when he neared his teen years, she too feared she would no longer be able to help him. By then at least, he possessed a sensible enough head to keep his feelings to himself. He found it tough to be without the loving company he never really knew he had and he could not determine the source of the new emptiness that he felt.

Like Manuun, Kentu learned with remarkable speed. He found himself always at the top of his class and always eager to learn more. His teachers discouraged this excellence by warning that moving faster than everyone else would not get him to his destination any quicker. Though this could not discourage his academic achievement, he found that these statements contained a great deal of truth to them. Every step in his life up to that point came neatly delivered to him and every step he took after that followed suit. The educational analysts deemed him suitable for a business job so they enrolled him in courses which prepared him for this predetermined future. During the latter half of his education, he met a girl by the name of Lattia. She wore her hair in long, spiraling curls and painted her lips and eyes with intense, pink makeup. They all wore the same uniforms even at this age – boys in slacks and tucked in shirts, girls in blouses and frilly skirts – but she seemed to fill her clothing particularly well. Kentu longed for the times when the teacher called upon her for an answer so that he could hear her sultry, disinterested voice. Eventually, he built up the courage to speak with her on the way to class.

"Lattia," he called ahead to her, while he brushed his black hair to the side and quickened his steps.

"Kentu, right?" she confirmed in that voice which made his knees weak.

"Yeah, that's me. You on your way to class?"

"Where else would I be headed," she asked, never once looking him in the eyes.

"Right, yeah, well I just figured maybe you'd like to go there together."

"It only makes sense to, you being here with me now and us needing to go to the same place."

"Oh, yeah sure. What about after class," his hands clutched the straps of his black backpack.

"I will be going to my next class which you're not in, so you will not be following me there."

"I didn't mean right after, of course, I just meant sometime after. I just thought maybe we could spend some time...you know...together – as opposed to separate, alone."

"Don't be odd," she sneered.

"Right, I'm sorry, I just –"

"Don't be sorry," she interrupted, "just be normal."

Then the conversation dropped. They entered into their Business Finance classroom and took their seats across from one another. He no longer admired the delicate curves of her face, nor did he so much as peek at her bulging bosom. For so long, he had an image of her as someone that could make all of his pain and loneliness go away. He thought she might be different – like him, but now he felt foolish for thinking such a thing.

He eventually accepted his diploma in an utterly silent and lifeless ceremony. Then he transferred into his Financial Assistant job which proved to be even more silent and lifeless. Lattia worked in the legal department of the same company, but she served as little more than a familiar face to Kentu. The job came with an apartment which he considered enormous, though in truth it was quite small and only large by comparison to his dormitories. He could now access a television monitor and all the music he could ever dream of listening to, but nothing that played could ever fill the void. In the years since the Legacy System came into being, the council stripped even more words from the language. No piece of modern literature, music, or cinema included references to feelings, especially that of love. Sometimes programs presented anger and chaos as enemies to tranquility, but not many other references to emotions could ever be found. Love ceased to exist in mainstream society, though making love certainly did not. One evening, Lattia stopped by and knocked on Kentu's door.

The young demigod's eyes widened at the sight of her in his doorway. She had her thick hair pulled elegantly over her shoulder and wore a tight, stretchy, orange dress which she filled out far better than any school uniform. She also came with bright, silver jewelry around her neck and ears. Her appearance dazzled him.

"We may spend time together now," she announced. "It would be an acceptable thing to do. We're adults now, after all."

He changed into a silky shirt, snug pants, and shiny shoes before following her out of his apartment building. They hopped into her sleek, pink car and drove to the nearest nightclub – he unable to peel his eyes off of her while they sped down the streets. He entered into the enormous building holding her hand and looked in awe at the vibrant lights which twirled about. Some tables lined either side of this great hall, but Lattia led him right to the sprawling dance floor. Thumping music blared through the air around them as they danced together. Lattia closed the gap between them hastily. She grabbed the back of his neck and wiggled her hips against his. Her firm breasts pressed against his chest. He felt an odd sensation swelling within him – one which filled the emptiness that plagued him for so long. He let his body rock to the rhythm of the beat and allowed her to touch him wherever she wished. He found that she too had no issue with when he stroked her hair or even when he cupped his hands under her breasts while she scooted her buttocks against his crotch. After hours of moving together like this, Kentu scampered alongside her back to the car where she drove them to his apartment and to his delight, she followed him inside.

He did not understand that she came here only for one goal. He saw tonight as the realization of all he ever hoped and dreamed about her. He thought she finally loved him. Though he had no concept of love, he could now feel the burning sensation inside of him that he chased after all his life. He grinned boyishly when she shoved him onto the couch and sat straddling his lap. Her lips dove down to meet his and her hands grabbed greedily at his dense shoulders and thick back. He wrapped his arms around her waist and squeezed the round musculature of her rear. She slid his shirt off and tossed it across the room. He kissed her some more before she pulled away and pointed to her back with a mischievous smirk. He felt around with his hands until he discovered the zipper, realizing it was his turn to take something of hers off. He slid it down to her lower back.

Then she stood with her hands held out and hoisted him to his feet where she tore the tube dress down over her breasts and let it fall to the floor – her high-heeled feet pushing it away. Then she kicked her silver shoes off and undid his pants. He kissed her neck and chest while they stood together in their underwear. She waited patiently for him to remove her bra, but it seemed she needed to lead him every step of the way. She wondered how he could be so slow with such a simple task, but then she remembered he was odd and probably did not watch many of the videos which made such things easier.

"Well," she hummed after a while of suspense. She made another gesture to her backside where his hands searched around once more for what she wanted. He came upon the clip, but could not manage to get it undone. "In then out," she advised, but he still fumbled with the mechanism.

"Have you really never done this before?" She snarled.

"Done what?" Kentu huffed innocently.

"Have you never been with a lady?"

"I'm with you right now. I was with you in school too."

"No, I mean *with* someone."

"I don't –"

"Have you ever had sex with a lady?" she snapped.

"Have you ever had sex with a gentleman?" he questioned. He knew the fundamentals of intercourse, but of course never experienced it himself.

"YES!" she exclaimed throwing her hands up in the air. She took a couple steps back and undid the bra clip herself. "Many times, I'm not really sure why you are just learning to do it now," she sneered tossing the garment aside.

"Wait!" he gasped, holding his hands up in the air while she approached. "I thought –"

"What?" She looked to him with her hands on her hips and a scowl across her face.

"I thought this was special, I thought we were going to be together."

"We're together right now, you moron! Seriously, what's wrong with you? Did you think we were going to become some exclusive thing?"

"Well, no I just – I –"

"Oh no you really did. Listen, Kentu, I'm going to give you the chance to act normal for once in your life. You can take off my panties and then drop those shorts and we will finish off this night. In the morning, I will be gone and we will probably never do this again, but I will take some pride in knowing that I fixed you for other partners. Is that clear to you?"

"I don't want this," he sighed, falling to the couch. "I want something else, something more."

"What else could you possibly want? Do you want a male? The way you look at me always made me think not, but hey if that's what you want, just go for it."

"That's not it."

"What then?" she practically yelled tossing her hands up into the air "What could be *more* than this," she hissed – motioning her hands down the length of her almost naked body.

"I don't know what it's called," he said in a hushed tone, "but it's missing."

"You know what, whatever! I tried to do a good thing here. I was really patient, Kentu. I knew this might be a bad idea, but I thought to myself, gee the poor guy's been staring at me this long, why not just give him a fantastic night even if he's weird. But you – you are just beyond help, good luck with not sleeping with anyone, ever, hope its real fun for you. Maybe in your next life you won't suck at this or be such a freak."

She threw her clothes back on and stormed out the door which hissed shut behind her. Kentu sat alone and in utter silence. He curled up on the couch and just lay there for the rest of the night. He wondered if he just made the biggest mistake of his life. Would sleeping with her have made all of his distress go away? Would it have made him less lonely? The more he thought about it the better he felt. He wanted her forever, not just for a night. If he could not have her for life, he did not want her at all. But still the heartbreak persisted. He eventually let it carry him into slumber. His parents watched from up above, desperate for a way to soothe his pain. They realized the only way to end his suffering was to tell him the truth about his existence, even if they could not be sure of his readiness for it. That next night, Teylaan opened a portal into Kentu's apartment for Yeb to go through. The light god sat on a plush chair and waited for his son to return from work. When Kentu stepped through the door and saw Yeb sitting in his home, his limbs froze in place. He vaguely recognized Yeb's face. Something about it made him feel comfortable and safe, but he had no idea why he felt that.

The god arose with his arms outstretched. Kentu inched into their embrace finding in them what he could find nowhere else. He returned his father's hug for a while, never wanting what he now felt to leave him. When Yeb finally let go, he helped the stunned demigod to a seat on the couch. That is where he explained it all to him. He started with the birth of the gods, a story long forgotten by the world. Then he explained the story behind Manuun's birth and early death. He described the banishment of the gods and the rise of their betrayer. He laid out for Kentu all that went wrong in the world and turned it from a place of love and community – a place of building – to the world that Kentu grew up in. He revealed that Kentu came from the remains of Manuun and that his half-god nature is why the treatments did not work on him. He also explained how Yeb and Rila visited Kentu as a babe to try and ease his suffering. Then he explained why they placed him into this world. He told him of the coming cataclysm which promised to lay claim to all those that Tubu corrupted and to destroy any good that persisted. Kentu had his mission now, whether he was ready for it or not.

"Where do I start?" the demigod asked.

"Head first to the Knight Rider factory in Wakan. There you will meet the workers who are known only to a select few as the Keeran Knights. They will be your first allies in this mission. Tell them who you are. They will believe you and they will be ready to fight by your side."

"Are you so certain I can fight?"

"Your essence is your own, but your body was Manuun's – I am certain that when the time comes, you will possess the means to fight. Good luck my son, I will be watching over you and come to your aid should you need it. I love you."

"I love you too," Kentu replied. *Love*, this is what he sought after, this is what he missed.

Yeb departed through Teylaan's portal which closed behind him. Kentu packed a bag filled with clothing and drove off in his navy car toward Wakan. He wondered if the Keeran Knights were like him – wondered if they could love. If others in this world could feel the way he felt, then he would do anything to save them.

Cataclysm

Kentu arrived in Wakan without much trouble. All of the checkpoints believed his story about wanting to purchase a Knight Rider from off the lot – that he always had a fondness for their bikes and wanted a really nice one for himself. He arrived at the manufacturing warehouse where the Keeran Knights took refuge from the world. He parked in front of the staggeringly obtuse building and walked into the pearly white sales area where the most current models of their bike lines stood on rotating display stands.

"Good afternoon," a dashing young salesman called to Kentu as he entered. "I'm Jalen, how can I help you today?"

Kentu eyed the gentleman carefully. He had light brown hair cropped close to his head and spiked in the front. He wore a classic black coat with a white shirt underneath and straight-legged black pants. His eyes sparkled like credits and his smile made it look like he already won this sale.

"I'm not here for a bike," Kentu mumbled.

The smirk dropped from the male's face. "What else would you come for?" he asked in a hushed voice.

"I'm looking for a Knight – the kind you can talk to rather than ride."

"I see," Jalen hummed. "Come with me then, I think I know just what you need."

The salesman led Kentu to the back of the sales area and down a narrow hallway. He fiddled with the buttons on his jacket a bit while they walked further into the compound. Then he stopped abruptly and shoved a blaster into the air. The new type of gun that he held was far more efficient than the firearms originally used to kill their founder's immortal father. Kentu froze in place, not sure what he should do.

"Who are you?" Jalen demanded.

"I'm Kentu. Yeb told me I should come here and talk to you about getting some help. Please put that away."

"Yeb? As in the god Yeb?"

"I know him better as my father, but yes."

"Father? He and Rila bore another child?"

"More like they sent their first son into the Legacy Machine and now here I stand Manuun, but not Manuun as I understand it."

"The clever gods!" Jalen nearly shouted, putting his pistol away. "I'm so sorry, my brother," he exclaimed, wrapping Kentu in a warm embrace. "We've waited for this day for generations, but I needed to be sure you were not someone who meant us harm."

"I need your help," Kentu persisted, though he returned the hug.

"My Knights are here for you, son of Yeb. I am the Knight Commander."

"It's an honor," Kentu said as Jalen released his hold.

"You must not fully understand what it is you must do, am I right?"

"Yes, it's all new to me, I just –"

"Don't fret!" Jalen consoled. "My men and I know exactly what must be done."

Yeb and Rila watched as Jalen closed up shop and summoned his army of eighteen into the warehouse. Kentu discovered the fleet of exquisite bikes which sat hidden in the bowels of the warehouse. Jalen showed him how to operate the vehicle which lit up and hummed to life at the demigod's touch. He looked around while the Knights fired up their transports. Jalen sent his crawling up next to Kentu's and handed him two sabre handles.

"My warriors prepared some weapons for you. Twin swords used to be your arsenal of choice."

"Thank you," the demigod replied.

"Someone alert the family units that we're mobilizing. We head for the Keeper Hideouts and then for the heart of the world. Open the gates!" The enormous bay doors glided open, allowing Solan's light to pour into the wide garage. "Just follow our lead, son of Yeb," Jalen said before propelling forward.

The bikes whipped out into the streets and soared toward their destination in one long line. They stopped first at the Wakan hideouts where they gathered Seekers by the car-full until all three safe houses were cleared out. Then Jalen sent two of his Knights to escort them to the inner ring and then to where the dark tower stood. Rila promised them long ago that the tower of the gods would return to crush the structure of their enemies and so they went there on faith. Then Tubu took notice of their activity from the depths of his chasm. He unleashed the endless hoard of dark creatures which he hid there. He meant to wait just a little longer, but the small pockets of the faithful forced his hand. Teylaan saw the shadow-spawn legion emerge into the world from his workshop. All the filled burial urns now rested within Digitarum – he and Timku finished sending them through only a short time ago. The grand inventor hurried out of his empty mortuary to alert the other gods. Now that Tubu's forces mobilized, they needed to lower their home back down to the world and join it for the end of days. The entire pantheon, save for Teylaan and Timku, set to disintegrating the floating plane and slowly bringing the tower down to the ground.

Teylaan and Timku initiated their rescue mission. Nine necropolises stored the remains of those who died faithful to the gods and they needed to be saved. A portal opened first in Litso. Timku leapt out of the swirling doorway and twirled about with his sickles outstretched. The guards that stood nearby fell into piles of steaming black polygons while the other necropolis guards opened fire on the intruder. Timku blinked behind them and sliced one of them down with his razor-edged blades before teleporting over to the other and taking him out as well. With the room cleared, he scooped up all the jars he could fit into the belt Rica made him. It had holsters all around the side and back of his legs for him to slide these containers into. Then he gathered however many else he could carry in his arms, returned to the tower, ascended to the primordial egg's shrine, and sent the remains through. He continued this process until the necropolis held no more of the god's faithful and then Teylaan closed the portal – opening a new one in a new necropolis. Timku had one down and eight more to complete.

Meanwhile, Kentu and the Knights busied themselves with trying to clear out the hideouts in the city of Kinran. Kentu found that while his entrance into Wakan went smoothly, his exit from there did not. The city officials tried to crack down on the unauthorized traffic out of the city, but Jalen's followers made short work of those that manned the checkpoints.

"Should we really just kill them like that?" Kentu asked the Knight Commander.

"They've died many times over, their essence now belongs to the Lord of Darkness – they can't be saved."

When Kentu saw their ashes turn to molten black goo, he accepted the explanation and rode alongside the warriors. Their shining black bikes cruised down the road connecting the two cities, their neon blue lights leaving light-streaks behind as they sped through the darkening landscape. When they arrived at their destination, the army of the nine cities already mobilized against them and Tubu's dark beasts bounded toward civilization. Kentu provided them with a healthy head start, but Teylaan saw from above that it would not be enough.

He scurried out of the work shop and flew out of the tower where the other gods steadied it downward. He warned both Yeb and Rila that they did not have enough time to clear out all the Keepers and dead at this rate. He helped them land the tower upon its old resting spot and crush the tower that rose up to take its place. The puny replacement structure fell to rubble with all those caring for it fleeing toward the inner ring of cities. Now that the tower of the gods sat in its rightful place once more, the gods' real work began. Teylaan sent Rila through to the outer cities to help her son rally the Seekers. Yeb joined in this effort while Rica and Garta awaited Teylaan's instruction. The twins stood watch at the towers base, ushering in their faithful and cutting down any that bore Tubu's taint. Teylaan rifled through images of the cities and even set up Yeb's orb so that he could look upon two images at the same time. Timku cleared out two more necropolises during this time, but they simply could not seem to work fast enough.

Kentu and Jalen had Kinran nearly evacuated when a hovercraft floated down into the streets. It opened fire on them while soldiers slid down ropes to ground level. Jalen sent the Seekers away with two more of his warriors while they opened fire upon the aircraft and armored troopers. Suddenly a grenade fell upon the wing of the angular craft and blew it apart. The rest of the ship crashed into a building, causing it to collapse upon some of the soldiers and pedestrians. As Kentu looked up, he saw long, white strips of cloth fall from the buildings around them and then lightly clad ladies slipped down from the building tops. They wore one piece lingerie dance suits with calf-high heeled boots and small white gloves. While they spiraled down the white cloth strips, they peppered the air with their silver automatic ray-guns. Their twisting decent from the buildings made it hard for the soldiers to hit them and their lethal precision mowed down the council's minions with little effort. Kentu spotted fifteen of them in total when they all set foot on the ground.

"Quite an entrance," the demigod mumbled, his eyes resting on the silver-haired matriarch that led them over to where the Knights took cover. The lady wore dark purple lipstick and eye shadow which gave her a fierce look. She approached Jalen with a smile and a hug.

"Matriarch Nara and the Daughters of Rin," Jalen introduced. "They are ladies of unmatched beauty and deadly grace."

"An honor," Kentu stated with a bow of his head.

"Jalen is this –?" The matriarch gasped seeing the sabre handles that the demigod clutched.

"This is Kentu – rather Manuun reborn as another."

"The honor is mine, then!" she exclaimed giving him a deep bow at the waist.

Kentu found the warmth of her voice and her glowing smile to be a comfort amidst the chaos. This peace did not last long, though. Soon screams resounded in the distance. Jalen twisted around to face his Knights.

"We're running out of time! We ride on!"

Then silver cars whipped around the corner, their passenger doors opening upward for the Daughters to climb inside.

"May I borrow the son of Yeb a while?" the matriarch asked turning to Jalen.

"See you in a bit!" he chirped

The Knight Commander rode off with his warriors and the Matriarch's sisters drove away in another direction. Nara slid her hand across Kentu's shoulder blades as she walked around him. She looked into his eyes for a moment before one corner of her mouth curled upward.

"It is said that before his death, Manuun fought side by side with our Matriarch during the great battle against the darkness. I would like to live such a moment with you now. Our forces need some time and I wish to buy it for them. Will you lend me your aid?"

"I will," Kentu promised while he activated the blades – their sharp energy shot out from the hilts.

They stood together in the streets as civilians shrieked and fled from the large, lanky beasts that pursued them through the grid of towering buildings. Nara held her blaster in one hand and an energy dagger in the other. The shadow-spawn came barreling toward them at a ravenous speed. Without even thinking much about it, Kentu charged forward to meet them. His hands glowed as he swung his swords to chop off the hands that swiped at him. Nara fired bolts through the monsters' screeching heads. They came with tails this time which swung about and nearly knocked Kentu off his feet a couple of times. He managed to dodge each assault with circular evasions and cut his foes down with slashes and stabs. Nara thinned out the writhing hoard and drove her knife through any that came to close to her. Black ash lay strewn across the ground yet they remained overwhelmed no matter how many fell to them.

When all seemed hopeless, Teylaan's portal popped open nearby loosing Garta and Rica upon the monsters. The god of strength wore a full suit of plated armor along with a helmet with flaring wings popping out of it. The goddess came in a firm breastplate over a mail shirt with a battle skirt over leggings and armored boots. Her braided hair slashed through the air as she leapt about. The two enjoyed the thrill of combat one more time together. Garta heaved his axe through the air while Rica pounced upon their foes.

"Go!" the goddess commanded, stepping toward them and swiping an arm to her side before turning back to the beasts.

Kentu retracted his energy blades and slid the grips into his red jacket. He ran toward the Matriarch and rushed her toward his bike. As they made their escape, Tubu came soaring through the air in a mass of bubbling, black fog. The pair stopped short just before the god of darkness dove toward them. Kentu pushed Nara behind him and crouched low, throwing his glowing hands up in front of him. A round force-field of light shielded him from Tubu's attack and repelled him backward. The blow knocked Tubu out of his foggy form. He fell against the ground in his natural body, stunned that the young demigod had the power to repel him like that. Kentu pulled the Matriarch along by the hand toward the bike. He leapt on top of it – the vehicle lighting up as soon as he took hold of its handles. They shot forward through the city – Kentu's swept bangs bouncing and Nara's loose hair flapping in the air as they sped toward another metropolis. They found that most of the army no longer focused on them, but instead turned their attentions to the shadowy beasts, so they cleared the checkpoints without any trouble.

Tubu arose from his flattened posture and snarled in a deep, vibrating growl which shook the air around him. He morphed back into the foggy haze and flew up into one of the battleships which fired at his monsters from the air. He slaughtered the crew with nothing but his sharp fingers and took a seat by the pilot. His red eyes stared into those of the frightened male at the controls.

"Turn this ship around," he seethed.

The pilot did as instructed without question or resistance of any kind. Tubu's hypnotic gaze guided the aircraft's operator to where Kentu fled on his bike, with Nara sitting behind him. The demigod felt safe in the grip of the Matriarch – like he could accomplish anything with her behind him. As it turned out, he would need to pull off some death defying feats after all as the ship's cannons opened fire on them. Beams of light exploded, tearing enormous holes in the smooth inter-city road. Kentu swerved from side to side in random patterns to evade the fire. Tubu placed a hand over the pilot's and made him push the throttle forward. The pointy ship roared over the pair's heads and shot forward a distance before curling around to face them. It let bolts loose upon them forcing Kentu to do a full three hundred and sixty degree spin on the bike to avoid the barrage. Then he rode forward under the belly of the cruiser where Nara fired up into it and set off an explosion in its light-core engine. It burst into pieces, but not before Tubu squirmed out in his gaseous form. Nara pressed her forehead against the back of Kentu's shoulder as they cruised forward, finally out of harm's way for a time.

Meanwhile, the other outer cities faced the same type of assault. Teylaan sent Shira and Shirun into one to keep it clear while their brother hastened to save those trapped inside its necropolis. The twins helped the last of the city's Keepers reach the road which led into Taran when the portal reopened for them. They stepped in knowing Timku's work was finally complete there and they arrived in the workshop only to be sent back out to where Timku now operated. Teylaan opened a gateway for Garta and Rica to return so that he could then send them to hold ground elsewhere now that Kinran had nothing left for them to preserve. The inventor then opened one for Yeb to come through.

"You must give what we talked about a try," Teylaan advised.

Yeb ripped off his plated shirt. He looked out the window of Teylaan's workshop to see the dark fog rolling in across the sky.

"You think I can do this?" Yeb huffed?

"Your son has already demonstrated that there is greater power lying within the ability to control light than we realized. You can do this, you must do this."

Yeb nodded to his advisor and flew out of the tower into the looming clouds which formed above them. As he flew higher and higher, the glow from his hands extended up his arms, across his shoulders and spread across his torso and face. His brilliance pierced the burning darkness of the swirling fog, allowing him to find Solan's light still shining above the black veil.

"It is time to come home," Yeb whispered as he summoned the being out of the orb of light and took his shining form up in his arms.

He descended back through the clouds and carried him to the tower's top. Yeb very nearly sent him through the egg when Solan wheezed out a "Wait! I have some power yet within me."

Yeb nodded graciously and left Solan by the swirling egg-shaped energy. The light god withdrew his boomerangs from their holster in his belt before landing nimbly against the ground – his body still radiating light. The people rushed past him into the tower where they began their long ascent to its top. Yeb kept watch for the evil that he knew would soon arrive.

Utter chaos reigned in the outer cities where the army and police forces of the people fought off the shadowy beasts. The last pockets of the Seekers sped out from the city, not realizing that the invisible Rila sat atop the car's roof. Two bikes ridden by the Knights escorted them out of the crumbling city, but then a pack of the creatures poured out in front of them. The vehicles came to a screeching stop as the monsters let loose a horrid cry into the space. Rila leapt from her perch and un-cloaked herself for all to see. As she rolled through the air, she took hold of her long spear and drove it into one of the creatures blocking her people's path. Then she spun about and thrust it into another before slinging it behind her and slicing an attacking monster clean in half. A portal opened up for her and she stepped inside leaving her bewildered followers to continue. Timku gathered up the last of the necropolis hostages from the six outer cities and returned to where Teylaan stood with Rila.

"Some of the Knights have fallen," Teylaan announced.

"Then send us to them," Timku demanded.

He and Rila charged through the portal and into the destroyed city streets. Timku summoned the fragments to himself while Rila fended off the creatures. They returned together and repeated this process several times before Timku could return to his work on the remaining necropolises.

By now the faithful folk were all piled up in the tower, ascending it in one long line and helping each other along while the gods gathered outside of it in preparation for the final stand. The Knights and Daughters pulled up to where the structure stood in waiting and took up a place with the gods as they prepared to do for centuries. Kentu and Nara drove through Arket – the place giving off a familiar quality despite its many changes over the years and the panic that now poured through its streets.

"This is where it happened," Nara shouted into his ear. "This is where you grew, where they ended your life."

The demigod nodded, glad to have an explanation for what he felt. His thoughts drifted to Lattia – the lady who could never love him back yet he still felt somehow connected to. She spent her final moments in bed with a muscular, young executive. When they finished their affair they glanced out the window to see the monsters slithering up the sides of their buildings and tackling the gunships out of the sky. One such beast came up to their window and slashed its claw through the bedroom wall – ending their existence. Kentu did not know of her end, nor would he ever know exactly how she came to death after lifetimes of rebirth. He worried for her, but knew what fate awaited her and that he could do nothing to change it. So he turned his focus back to the task at hand – back to the lady whose arms wrapped around his torso tightly.

They pulled up to the tower just as Timku finished gathering the very last of the deceased prisoners. They joined the others and Timku sent the remaining fragments into Digitarum. The god of death returned to his mentor who looked on at the world through his globes.

"All is ready," he said softly. "You did well, my boy."

"We all did," Timku corrected. "Make sure the rest of the folk make it into Digitarum."

Teylaan grabbed his pupil by the shoulder and pulled him into an embrace before bowing his head and leaving his workshop, knowing he would never return to work here again. Timku floated down to where the gods waited alongside the Keeran Knights and Daughters of Rin. They watched as Tubu's forces tore through the nine cities and rushed upon them. The Cataclysm was over, but the final stand had not yet begun.

Digitarum

Teylaan shouted for the folk to make haste while the other gods fought outside. Shira brought her hammer down upon their foes while Shirun's axes cleaved through them. Both wore full suits of shimmering armor and helmets like their father's. They stayed close to one another, fighting back to back when things got too heavy. The light of Yeb's body and the small lights in the tower were all that sheltered them from the darkness that rolled in. Kentu contributed what light he could, though he was not able to match the radiance of his father. The Daughters and Knights pierced their dark surroundings with bolts of energy which shredded through Tubu's forces. The seemingly endless expanse of his army flooded toward them with unrelenting ferocity.

Yeb hurled his boomerangs from above – his energy coursing through them and making the weapons radiate light. Kentu twisted his swords through the air with Nara and Jalen following close behind to thin out a path for him. Rila poked her massive spear through several of the beasts at a time before cracking it down upon another. Garta and Rica fought closer together than ever – their bodies practically acting as one. Garta swung his axe high while Rica skewered their enemies with low strikes. They stepped around each other in perfect harmony. No shadow-spawn could get near them or had any hopes of tearing them apart from one another. The gods fended off Tubu's beasts as well as they could, yet no end came to the onslaught. Knights and Daughters started to fall to the lethal claws of the swarm. Timku caught their fragments and put them into the vases that he loaded into his large belt.

Off in the distance, they saw Tubu barreling toward them in a smoky cloud. He smashed against the ground and morphed into his normal form. This was the first time that the gods saw him directly since his first attack on them. They did not realize that his skin color changed into the steaming grey hue that now covered him. He barred his white teeth at them and let loose a hollow cackle. He threw his arms up into the air and his beasts seemed to stop their assault for a while. Timku took the opportunity to ascend to the towers top to send the urns through and restock his belt. The other gods tightened their perimeter and what remained of their mortal following drew closer to the tower's base.

"You see Yeb? Is this not more fun? Can you not see the beauty in this destruction?"

"Tubu stop this!" the light god called back. "If you continue, there will be nothing left. Do not do this." Yeb did not really think he could dissuade Tubu from his plans, but hoped to stall him for as long as he could.

"Yes, everything must go, but it is good – let me show you. The darkness is not to be feared, Yeb. It is very beautiful and powerful – it is our destiny – I have seen this!"

"No, Tubu, we were meant for so much more. You have had your destruction, now stop this, while there is still a little left of this world."

"NO!" He shrieked. "I will not let you keep what is left from me! I have come too far – the rest of this world belongs to me! It must become part of the darkness!"

"Then it seems we were always doomed to fight one another," Yeb sighed.

Up above, Teylaan watched the folk file into the egg's portal to Digitarum. Solan looked below to see the endless hoard surround the forces of light. He saw the argument between Yeb and Tubu and noted that it seemed to go by quicker than needed. Any second now, Tubu's army would fall upon those at the tower's base – they needed help to flee. Solan's body still coursed with energy so he took a couple of steps back and sent bolts of light into the chest-high wall. It fell to the ground in disintegrating chunks while Solan secured the gold-colored loin cloth which Teylaan brought up to him. Then he sprinted forward and leapt from the tower. His body radiated as he plummeted through the air. He landed on his feet, surviving the fall without any injury and smashed his fist into the ground. A shockwave of light shot out of his body and burnt through the ring of monsters. Tubu hissed and floated away in his aerosol form.

The explosion left Solan too weak to do anything more. He fell to the ground and Teylaan descended to scoop him up and send him to Digitarum. The gods readied themselves to defend the tower a little longer while Timku made a daring choice. If he could manipulate the matter of the dead, perhaps he could also levitate the living. He rose up into the air and called the Daughters, Knights, and demigod to himself. Then focusing all his thoughts on the task at hand, he managed to lift them all up to the top of the tower. Teylaan went inside and flew down a few floors to where the last of their refugees still made their escape. The gods made their ascent with Tubu's creatures clambering up the tower behind them. They knocked down what they could but the beasts scuttled up to the top in an endless stream. Timku ushered in the rest of the mortal warriors, with Jalen, Nara, and Kentu staying behind. The god of death descended to where Teylaan yelled for the people's haste. Out the window, he saw the shards of Tubu's fallen merge into giant tentacles with sharp ends. They writhed from where they sat rooted into the ground and heaved their pointed ends toward the tower.

Timku looked to his mentor wide-eyed. Teylaan knew that time ran out and he gave Timku a nod before flying up. The reaper threw his hands into the air – his fingers spread wide. The remaining folk were torn apart into ash which he dragged through the air up the spiraling staircase in a flowing tail. As he pulled them along, the razor-edged tentacles drove into the tower. The structure shook and started to fall apart as Timku sent the trail of disintegrated bodies straight into the swirling gateway to their new home. He hoped this new world would truly be their salvation as he shoved the stream of polygons into the orange plasma. Then the mortal leaders jumped in followed by Shira and Shirun. Garta and Rica went in next, dragging the exhausted Timku in with them. Then the tower buckled under the damage it sustained. It toppled over to the side while the creatures leapt upon the remaining gods with Tubu leading their final assault.

Teylaan slammed his staff against the tilted floor and distorted the flow of time. The tower's fall came to a near stop and Tubu's monsters barely glided forward. Even Tubu's progress slowed because of the warp. He stretched out an arm in slow motion as Rila flew into the egg. Yeb took one last look at their enemy.

"I am sorry you could not be saved as well," he said softly to Tubu before following Rila.

Then Teylaan entered through the gateway and time returned to normal. Tubu and his forces crashed into the egg which repulsed them. No matter how desperately the crashed against it, they found no point of entry. The tower crashed into pieces which shattered against the ground and the egg's light went out. Tubu lingered in the space above and took in the sight of all that he laid waste to. He seethed in anger at what his fellow gods managed to whisk away and that he was denied a full victory. Still, he had his destruction – he reveled in his darkness. He smiled at the sight of all that used to be but was no longer.

On the other end of the portal, Rila, Yeb, and Teylaan crashed into Digitarum – landing sharply against the ground. They discovered that no egg-shaped energy existed on this side. They stepped through a one way doorway and no voice could be summoned here, but perhaps that would be just fine. When they looked around they saw the magnificent golden towers of the eternal city. They took in the soft perennial glow that originated from no apparent light source and they felt the comforting warmth that surrounded all things. They saw all the people that they managed to save. Those who died reconstructed themselves before their eyes, including Rin who looked to them with a beaming smile. Adding to their delight, they found that no creature of darkness followed them. Then they noticed something curious. All the polygons peeled off of them and burnt up in the air, yet they retained their forms as beings of pure energy. They could take up any appearance they wished – could become their ideal image of themselves. A much younger-looking Keeran approached Jalen and the Knights from across the generations in a joyous gathering. Solan turned off his glow, finding no need for it here in this land of light. He reunited with Rila for the first time since he became one with the luminous orb. Kentu split apart, becoming both Manuun and Kentu at once. Manuun flew over to his parents, realizing that all could float about as the gods could. He locked into a tight embrace with Rila and Yeb. Rica, Garta, and their children huddled together as well – Timku motioning for Teylaan to join them. Kentu joined his family as well before he and Manuun sought out their matriarch allies. Manuun stood with Lira while Kentu held hands with Nara. They led the folk into the golden city where nothing but love, happiness, and peace could exist.

Their new world felt ephemeral rather than constant – it pulsed like an emotion. It felt strange to be here, to exist like this, but all felt that in time this would no longer be so. It seemed like they lived their whole lives lost in a wilderness and they finally found their way back home. Rin reunited with them and took pride in seeing all the females who dedicated their lifetimes to honoring her memory and continuing her work. None could want for anything more than they had now. They lamented the loss of their old world, but being here with so many saved from Tubu's destruction hardly felt like a loss. Yeb, floated high above the radiant city with Rin on his right and Rila on his left.

"This is it," Yeb announced. "The end to all pain and sadness."

"This is what we fought for," Rila added.

"This is home," Rin agreed.

I watch from my seat while the gods and their creation settle into Digitarum. This wasn't the outcome I hoped for, but somehow it seems better. None of my simulations ever ended in a perfect world being constructed no matter what I gave to or took away from them. This one ended in destruction like the others, but it also ended in something else. These people earned their place in Digitarum. They earned it with suffering, sacrifice, heroism, bravery, strength, speed, skill, and heart. They made use of every gift bestowed upon them and saved as many as they ever could have hoped to, perhaps more. Maybe no world could be perfect whether real or simulated...or both. As I look upon Yeb's face while it lights up on my screen, I can't help but think that this was all real in a way. It certainly was for the people inside of it and I think it might have been real for me too despite my role as a spectator. I'm not sure that this run brought me any closer to answering the question of what it would take for imperfect creatures to create a perfect world, but none ever brought me so close to tears as this one either. I am their creator and in some cases, an advisor. I told myself I would not interfere, but my love for these entities proved too great to remain indifferent. I am responsible for all things both good and evil, yet I never could have known just how intense this experience would become.

I send the world now under Tubu's reign to the depths of the archives, but I can't bring myself to shut down Digitarum. I take out an empty drive and move the file onto it. Then I plug it into a large, sub-processing machine where it can continue to run as long as my laboratory has power. I know I should continue this work, but for now, I want to take in what I've learned from these people and relish in their victory. Besides, with Digitarum now fully inhabited, I will need a new world to serve as the birthplace of future creations. Digitarum served as the seed for many other digital worlds, but now one returned to it and I'm not really sure how I should move forward – or IF I should move forward. Digitarum is where the process started and where this phase has ended – there will never be another place quite like it now that so many incredible persons dwell within it. It's a place that I hope will exist forever.

Derek Bailey

About the Author:

Derek Bailey is a graduate of Southern New Hampshire University's Game Design and Development Program (BA) where he also completed minor in Creative Writing. He is a graduate of the four year Honors Program, was President of the Game Design and Development Club, served as a Peer educator, and frequently acted as a lector during Sunday Mass on campus. He has a passion for storytelling in all forms and across a number of genres. He has ghostwritten a science fiction novel, but *Digitarum* is his true debut novel.